sammy keyes

AND THE curse OF moustache mary

sammy keyes

AND THE curse OF moustache mary

by WENDELIN VAN DRAANEN

SCHOLASTIC INC.
New York Toronto London Auckland Sydney
Mexico City New Delhi Hong Kong

ISBN 0-439-22286-9

Published by Scholastic Inc.,
555 Broadway, New York, NY 10012,
by arrangement with Random House Children's Books,
a divsion of Random House, Inc.

12 11 10 9 8 7 6 5 4   3 4 5 6/0

Printed in the U.S.A.   40

First Scholastic printing, May 2001

This book is dedicated to my parents,
Peter and Mieske Van Draanen,
who had the courage to pioneer wide waters and foreign soil
in search of a better life.

Also to my husband's great-great-grandfather,
Lyman Lysander Huntley,
whose journal of crossing the plains in 1850
is a historic treasure.

Grateful thanks to Nancy Siscoe for the fifteen pages
of editorial wisdom, and to my husband, Mark Parsons,
for fifteen years of spirited adventuring.

Thanks, too, to the following for research consultation:
Ann Parsons, Forensic Toxicologist
Eric Parsons, Supervising Criminalist
Ed Smith, Fire Cause Consultant
Ilona Dobbe, All Seasons Nursery

And finally, thanks to Jason Tamura and Jason Graham for
the brainstorming sessions; to Nicholas May—I've still got
your magazines; and to Mary-Mary Kuczkowski, Leslie Kuo,
and Susan Cavaletto for reviving my school-fried brain
at pow-wow lunches in the Cave.

sammy keyes

AND THE CURSE OF moustache mary

PROLOGUE

You'd think I could spend the night at a friend's house without finding myself knee-deep in pig poop. But no. I couldn't even *make* it there without practically breaking every bone in my body, and by the time the clock was gonging in the New Year, well, I was in so deep it was going to take a *backhoe* to get me out.

ONE

Marissa McKenze is the last person on earth you should ever accept a ride from. And I *knew* that. Trouble is, she had a bike, Holly had a bike, and all I had were my high-tops and the distant memory of a skateboard that had disappeared while I was playing video games at the mall.

And maybe I should have wobbled around on Holly's handlebars instead, but Holly wasn't offering. Marissa was. And since Dot's new house was clear out in Sisquane and I didn't want to spend all morning getting there, what choice did I have?

Actually, things were going pretty well. Our duffel bags were in back, bungeed tight and balanced right, and it was real foggy out, so Marissa was driving kind of carefully for once. We'd made it three whole blocks down Broadway and another three whole blocks down Cook Street without so much as a serious wobble. But then, just as I was starting to relax a little, these guys come barreling down a cross street on skateboards.

Holly stopped. Just locked up her brakes and slid to a halt. Marissa, on the other hand, *started* to stop, but then changed her mind and decided to *go*. And as we're heading for the collision of the century, she lets go of the handlebars and cries, "Timber!"

3

She goes down sideways, and I sail through the air, straight for this guy who's ducking and weaving on his skateboard, trying to avoid me. But I'm flying at him like a human cannonball, and he doesn't have a chance. Not a prayer. I nail him, *smack!* right to the asphalt.

His skateboard goes flipping off, and his mouth does, too, letting loose with a string of four-letter synonyms for Ouch!

I untangle myself from him and hold on to my arm, because it hurts pretty bad and blood's already seeping through my sweatshirt. He's still swearing away, kind of dancing around flicking a wrist, but he interrupts himself long enough to say, "Stupid females!"

I sit there in the middle of the street holding my arm, trying to contain the pain. "I'm sorry. I...I..."

"You what?" he snaps. "You thought you could ride around town like a circus act and people would stop and cheer?"

Blood's starting to ooze through the right knee of my jeans, and since my whole body's pretty sore from having had an asphalt adjustment, I don't feel like arguing or explaining. I just sit there with my eyes closed and say, "Look, I'm sorry, okay? I'm sorry."

Then I hear someone laughing. So I look up from my private little spot in the middle of the street and what do I see? A guy with brown hair and baggy pants on his way to becoming hysterical about bruised-up bodies in the street. And I'm about to tell Baggy Boy to shut up when I hear someone *else* laughing behind me. I turn around, and there's Marissa and the guy she'd crashed into, dusting off, laughing. And then there's Holly, straddling her bike with her hand in front of her mouth, about to bust up, too.

Well. Obviously they're all just fine. And I suppose I was, too, only I wasn't ready to admit it yet. I was too mad. Mad at Marissa for being such a bad driver. Mad at my mother for buying me a pink angora sweater for Christmas instead of something I wanted—like a new skateboard or a bike. And the more I sat there, the madder I got, and the more I wanted to kill the guy who'd stolen my skateboard in the first place. I mean, if I still had it, I wouldn't be sitting there in the middle of the street all banged up from riding around town like a circus act.

Then I hear Marissa's victim say, "You don't remember me, do you?"

Marissa looks at him a little closer, then says, "Oh, yeah...you're..."

He helps her out. "Taylor. You asked me for directions the first day of school, remember?"

Well, *I* recognize him. He's Taylor Briggs, slick-and-slimy eighth grader. Good friends with Heather Acosta, red-and-rotten seventh grader. Taylor's older brother is best friends with Marissa's cousin Brandon; Taylor's the one who told Heather about Marissa being rich, and Taylor's the one who told Heather that I looked like a *fourth* grader.

Now, Heather may be cat hair in my craw, and there's probably not a kid at William Rose Junior High who doesn't know that truth to her is a foreign language—one she's not about to learn. But that first day of seventh grade, when she told me that Taylor thought I looked like a fourth grader, you could tell—there was truth behind it.

So I'm sitting there, mad at the world, mad at Marissa for laughing with a guy who's friends with Heather and thinks I look like a fourth grader, when Baggy Boy comes up to the guy I'd bombed and hands him back his skateboard. "Here you go, Snake. You all right?"

He says, "Yeah, dude. Thanks," and gives me one last glare.

I'm sitting there thinking, Snake? What kind of stupid name is Snake? when I notice the bottom of his skateboard. It's a metal-gray color, but it's been spray-painted that way. And I can tell, because underneath, where the gray's been scraped away jumping curbs, it's purple. A light purple with dark veins running through it. Like it had been dipped in molten amethyst. And there's only one other board I've ever seen that looks like that.

Mine.

I get up and say, "Hey, wait a second!"

He turns around.

"Where'd you get that skateboard?"

He sneers at me. "Oh, now you want to learn to ride? Don't *even* go there." He looks over at Baggy for a laugh. "Walkin's more your speed."

He turns to go, so I say, "No really. Wait a minute. Where'd you get it?" I run up for a better look, and when I see the foot grip, it's like my heart hits rapids.

Along the back of the foot grip, there's a three-inch strip missing. A three-inch strip completely gone except for a little piece sticking out like Florida in a States puzzle.

So between Florida on the top and amethyst on the bottom, there's no doubt in my mind: That skateboard's mine. And suddenly I'm not feeling my banged-up bones or the blood trickling down my leg. I'm feeling mad. Branding-hot mad.

I close in on the guy, saying, "Where did you *get* it?"

He's looking at me like I've got something contagious. "I bought it off a friend, okay?"

I get right in his face. "Well, where did your *friend* get it, then?"

"Hey, back off, psycho!" He looks over at Taylor, then back at me. "At a garage sale, all right? Like it's any of your business."

"It *is* my business!" I twist the board and point to the band of purple. "This is *my* skateboard and I can prove it. I wrote my initials right up here."

He snickers. "I don't see no initials."

"Scrape off the paint."

He backs away from me, so I lunge for the skateboard. "I said, scrape off the paint!"

He wrestles it out of my hands. "You *are* psycho!"

I can't just let him walk away. That's *my* skateboard. And somehow I can't find it in me to reason with the guy or have a nice little chat about how the right thing for him to do would be to give it back. No, watching him walk off with my skateboard, there's only one thing left to do.

Jump him.

I go flying through the air to tackle him again, but this time he doesn't go down. He spins and bucks and finally just throws me off. "Dude! Get a grip!"

Marissa helps me up and whispers, "It isn't worth it, Sammy. It's only a skateboard."

"But it's *my* skateboard, and he knows it!"

Holly calls, "Yeah! Hey—that thing's pretty beat-up anyway. Why don't you scrape the paint off and settle this?" She shrugs. "Unless you're lying and *you* stole it."

Snake takes a step toward us. "Who you callin' a liar? You think I'd want to *steal* this thing?"

Taylor plants himself between us like a road-wrestling referee. "He is telling the truth. He bought it off me." He shrugs. "I got it at a garage sale for five bucks."

Well, that buttons my beak. Finally I choke out, "But it's *mine*."

Taylor gives me a sad little shake of the head. "If it was, it's not anymore."

Just then a primer-gray pickup truck with wide tires and huge sideview mirrors comes rumbling down the street. And the minute Taylor sees it, he practically stomps his foot. "Oh, maaaan…"

The driver cranks down the window and calls, "Get in. Mom and Dad want you back home."

There's also a guy in the back of the pickup, and he leans out and calls to Taylor, "Hop into the paddy wagon, bro. The gestapo's out in force."

Marissa whispers, "Is that Karl?"

I whisper back, "Who's Karl?"

"Brandon's best friend, remember?"

Now maybe it was, but the guy in the back of the truck wasn't anyone I recognized as being any kind of friend of Brandon's. I mean, I'd been to pool parties at Brandon's before, and this guy sure didn't look like anyone I'd ever seen him with.

Marissa whispers, "God, that *is* Karl. His hair's gotten long, and he looks…I don't know, *older*, but that's him."

Baggy Boy goes over and asks for a ride, and pretty soon Snake's on board, too, only none of them are in the cab. They're piled up like a load of cattle in the back, settling in as Big Brother grinds into gear and lets out the clutch.

So off they go into the fog with my skateboard. And all of a sudden my body's aching and I can feel the blood crusting my jeans to my knee, and all I want is to sit down and cry.

Marissa sees the sleeve of my sweatshirt and says, "Maybe we should take you to a doctor."

"I don't need a doctor!"

Holly comes over and says, "Let me see," and makes me pull my arm out of the sleeve. Marissa about faints when she sees the scrape, but Holly turns my arm back and forth and says, "You just need some gauze and tape. A doctor can't do anything for that."

I don't happen to have a box of gauze and a roll of tape handy, and I sure didn't want to go home to dig some up. But then Marissa asks, "Do you think Hudson will have some?"

Hudson! Of course! We were only a few blocks from his house, and if anyone in Santa Martina could patch me up, it was Hudson Graham.

Not that Hudson's a doctor or anything. He's seventy-two and retired—from what, I'm not real sure—but what

I do know is that he's a friend I can count on, and he's got the tools to fix anything. Including a scraped arm and a banged-up knee.

So off we went to Cypress Street to find Hudson. And I was expecting him to be in a chair on his big porch, sipping tea like he always is, but when we turned up the walkway, no Hudson.

I tried the bell, then peeked in the living room window. No Hudson. And I'm just about to give up when a jogger in gray sweats and white Nikes appears on Hudson's walkway.

He might have been able to fool me altogether if it weren't for those bushy white eyebrows sticking out like fog lights from beneath his sweatshirt hood. And even after I knew it was Hudson, it still felt strange. Like discovering that the jacket you've been wearing all year is reversible.

I mean, Hudson drinks iced tea, reads books, and spends his days on his porch watching the world go by. Hudson does not wear sweats. Hudson does not jog. And Hudson Graham does not wear tennis shoes. He wears boots. Cowboy boots. Red ones, green ones, furry ones, ones that look like the hide of a Tyrannosaurus rex— boots.

So seeing him appear out of the fog in tennis shoes and sweats spooked me.

He pulls back his hood and ruffles his beacon of white hair. "Sammy, are you all right? You look pale." Then he notices the sleeve of my sweatshirt. "Here. Come up here and sit down."

He gets me onto his porch and parks me in a chair, then asks, "What happened?"

I glance over at Marissa, who starts fidgeting around, doing the McKenze dance. "They came out of nowhere. And they were going so fast!" She looks up at me. "I couldn't help it!"

Hudson sizes up the number of wheels on his walkway and the number of people on his porch and says, "You riding tandem again?"

I scowl and nod, and pull my arm out of my sweatshirt. After he inspects it, he whispers, "I thought you swore off," and heads for the house.

I call after him, "I did! But Dot's moved out to Sisquane, and I can't exactly *walk* that far."

A minute later Hudson's back with a first aid kit, and while he's cleaning me up, I tell him about our little crash-dummy convention and how I wouldn't have to be riding on Marissa's handlebars if my skateboard hadn't been stolen.

When I'm all done, he says, "This whole situation could also have been avoided if you'd asked me for a ride." I keep twitching away from him, because he's scrubbing pretty good and it stings. But he pins my arm down and says, "I'm surprised your grandmother didn't insist." He eyes me. "She *does* know what you're doing, doesn't she?"

"She knows I'm spending the weekend at Dot's..."

One bushy white eyebrow arches up.

"And I told her Marissa was giving me a ride..."

His eyebrow arches up even higher. "But...?"

I look down and confess, "But I never told her that the *ride* Marissa was giving me was on her handlebars."

He studies me with a frown, then pops open some disinfectant and smears it all over my arm. "A vital piece of information conveniently omitted?"

"I didn't *lie*. I just didn't tell her."

Hudson doesn't say a word. He just puts gauze on my arm, wraps it up, and starts working on my knee. And I'm feeling bad, like I *did* lie. "Hudson, it was either go with Grams to visit Lady Lana or spend New Year's at Dot's. What would *you* have done?"

"Rita's gone to Hollywood?"

"Uh-huh. And she was really pushing for me to go with her." I scowl at him and mutter, "Like I want to start my New Year with a tour of the set they used for Lady Lana's GasAway commercial."

"Could've been interesting to see your mother's work environment."

"It would've been torture! Besides, seeing her for two days at Christmas was enough to last me for another year."

Hudson sighs and says, "I heard about your angora sweater."

"It's *pink*."

"I know." He tries to stifle a grin. "I guess I'd have chosen Dot's, too."

"Exactly."

Hudson snaps his first aid kit closed. "So let's get you there in one piece, shall we? I'd give you a ride, but I sense that being chauffeured is not what you had in mind."

"It's really nice of you, but I…"

"But you don't want a lift when your friends are riding."

I shrug. "Yeah."

Marissa and Holly have been kind of standing around, keeping quiet, but when Marissa hears that, she says, "Maybe our bikes would fit in the trunk?"

Hudson smiles. "I have a better idea."

He disappears down the side steps, and when he comes back, about ten minutes later, he's pushing a bike alongside him. Now this bike is old, but it's old like his car, Jester. Shiny old. Tons-of-chrome old. Whitewall-tires old. Way-too-cool-to-ride old.

I take one look at it and say, "You're kidding, right?"

"Not at all. What am I saving it for? It's just collecting dust."

"But what if I wreck it?"

He throws his head back and laughs. "Then you wreck it. It's seen a few adventures in its lifetime. A few more won't hurt."

So we divvied up the duffels and started off again, and let me tell you, I couldn't stop smiling. Hudson's bike was smooth and fast, and the wind in my face felt like something I hadn't known in ages. It felt like freedom.

But if I'd had any idea what we were riding toward, I'd have turned right around, returned the bike, and jumped the next train to Hollywood.

TWO

The last time I'd been to Sisquane was on a field trip in the fourth grade. In my mind it was kind of a hick town with a lot of weeds, sagging barns, and crooked trailers. But as we coasted down the road into Sisquane, I realized that a lot can change in three years. Instead of weeds and trailers, there were condos. And estates. And a sign for a *golf* course, coming soon.

I called over my shoulder, "Did we take a wrong turn?"

Marissa says, "No, this is right. Mom drove us out here looking at property last summer."

"You're kidding! She's thinking about moving out *here*?"

"Oh, you know Yolanda. She's always looking for something to buy. She never went back, though. I think there was too much dirt around for her."

Holly asks, "Dirt?"

Marissa grins. "Yolanda prefers cement." She pulls over and wrestles a folded paper out of the hip pocket of her jeans. "I'd better look at Dot's map. I think we're close, but I can't remember the name of the road."

We hover around her, checking out the map, then she taps it and says, "Right here. Meadow Lane." She wedges the map back into her pocket and off we go, past the

Spanish-style gateway for High Ridge Homes, past Pioneer Village Estates, past a water tower and half a mile of fields, down the hill to Meadow Lane.

The road's a *lane*, all right. It's narrow, overgrown, and *dirt*. But the name DEVRIES is written across a mailbox nailed to a post, so we all kind of shrug and say, "Let's go."

We wobble along single file, dodging potholes and gopher homes. Holly calls, "Why would anybody want to move out *here*?"

Marissa calls back, "Dot said they needed more room."

"Yeah, but good grief!"

"They're also starting a nursery."

"A nursery? Who'd want to bring their kid out here?"

Marissa laughs. "Not for babies...for plants!"

We round the bend and all of a sudden there's Dot's house. And it's big, all right. It's sprawled out, bumper to bumper with enormous oak trees, and has a porch that runs clear along the front.

Dot comes slamming through the screen door. "You're here! You're here!"

We all laugh because she's practically jumping up and down.

"Come on in! Park your bikes over here. Wow, I can't believe it! This is going to be so much fun! Are you hungry? Thirsty? Here, let me help you with your stuff. Who wants a root beer?"

Dot's old house was like the Land of Blue. Her family is Dutch, and it seems that everything they own has something blue about it. Blue curtains, blue dishes, blue carpet, blue cushions. Blue. And I don't know if I was expecting a little change of decor because this was a different house or if I was just figuring that they couldn't possibly have spread that much blue around in such a short period of time, but the fact is I was *way* underestimating the Power of Blue.

In the blue-wallpapered kitchen we found Mrs. DeVries weighing out flour onto a white cloth. On the blue-tile counter to one side of her were Dot's little sisters, patting white flour on each other's faces, and on the blue-linoleum floor snoring away was the sort-of-white family sheepdog, Nibbles. Mrs. DeVries looks up and says, "Your friends have arrived, Margaret?"

Dot says, "Yup!" then asks, "Are you making enough?"

Mrs. DeVries laughs. "*Ja,* I'm sure I am. Four times the recipe."

"Because this is Sammy. She eats a lot."

"I *do?*"

Dot winks one of her big brown eyes at me and says, "And this is Holly. *She* eats a lot, too." Holly pulls a face, but Dot just ignores her. "And this is Marissa. You wouldn't *believe* how much Marissa can eat."

Mrs. DeVries studies us for a minute, then says, "No, I wouldn't, but all right. Five times, *ja?*"

Dot says, "Yes! Thanks, Mom," and then whispers, "*Oliebollen* are my favorite. You wouldn't believe how many *I* can eat!"

We laugh, then Marissa asks, "What are *oliebollen?*"

Dot's mom transfers the flour from the cloth to a blue ceramic bowl. "A Dutch treat."

Dot adds, "We only get them on New Year's Eve."

By now Dot's sisters have graduated from patting flour to sprinkling it in each other's hair. And the sprinkling doesn't last long, either. Pretty soon they're bombing.

Mrs. DeVries cries, "Anneke! Beppie! Stop!"

They bomb each other one last time and then look at their mom like dusty little angels. "We only did a little."

"Go. Right now. Go outside and shake off. Then find your father and help *him* for a while."

They slip off the counter and giggle their way out the back door. Dot says, "Do you want us to help you, Mom?"

Mrs. DeVries pulls the salt carton off a shelf. "Maybe later. Why don't you show your friends around?"

Dot gives her a big smile. "Okay!"

"Oh, there is one thing you can do. Track down the *sjoelbak*. I haven't seen it since we moved. Ask your father. He might know."

"Okay. We'll find it!"

"Oh, and Margaret?"

"Yes, Mom?"

"Are you sure you want to stay in the carriage house? There's plenty of room inside..."

"It'll be more fun out there. More like camping!"

Marissa looks over at me and pulls a face, but she's too polite to say, Um, excuse me...but I'd rather be nice and cozy inside than sleep with bugs in the freezing cold, so she doesn't say a thing. She just drops her duffel in a corner with ours and follows us out the back door.

Dot's backyard isn't exactly a *yard*. It's more like a forest of oak trees. They're not bunched real close together or anything, they're just so old and large that they arch together into a giant green canopy. And there's no lawn covering the ground. There's a carpet of tan leaves instead. And it's thick. Like extra-plush, only crunchy. And as we're crunching our way across it, Dot says, "Dad's got to make a delivery for a big party up the road, so he's probably in one of the greenhouses."

Just past the oak canopy are two arched buildings sitting on the ground like enormous white cocoons. Dot smiles. "There they are."

Holly says, "Wow! Did your dad build those?"

"No. They were already here." Dot laughs. "Dad tells everyone we moved because we needed more room, but actually I think it's because his *plants* needed more room. They moved in way before we did!"

Dot opens the door to the first greenhouse, and we all peek inside as she scans the place for her dad. There are rows and rows of plants—I'm talking some are *trees*— and they go from one end of the cocoon to the other. And then, almost connecting with them, are philodendrons and ferns the size of laundry baskets hanging from the roof. It's like we've stepped into the steamy belly of a gigantic jungle-eating caterpillar.

Dot says, "There he is!" and heads off through the trees.

Mr. DeVries is adding plants to a long wooden pallet on wheels. He spots us and says, "Oh, hello, girls! You made it!"

Dot says, "You remember Marissa and Sammy from Halloween, Dad?"

Mr. DeVries grins. "You mean the Mummy and the Marsh Monster, *ja*?"

We laugh and say, "That's right!" Then Dot adds, "And this is our friend Holly."

Mr. DeVries says, "Glad you all could come."

Dot bounces up and down on the balls of her feet. "Mom asked us to find the *sjoelbak*. Do you know where it is?"

"In the basement, I think." He looks at his watch and asks, "Do you know where your *brothers* are?"

Dot shakes her head. "I thought they were helping you out here."

"They went off to find some rope, but it's been quite some time."

Dot says, "We'll help you, Dad," then she looks at us like, Won't we?

We give a chorus of "Sure, we'll help" and watch the knots in Mr. DeVries' face disappear. "Really? But this is supposed to be a day for you and your friends. You helped me plenty yesterday, hon."

We all shrug and say, "We don't mind," and then Dot says, "Tell us what to do."

"Well, let's get these plants to the truck. I've got a wagon of cut flowers in the other greenhouse. Bring them together outside and I'll back the truck up."

We'd barely gotten the wagons together when Mr. DeVries comes rumbling up in the delivery truck. Now this is not a truck like you're used to seeing. It's a panel truck, but it's got screened windows for vents along the back, and it's green. Bright, sour apple green. And there

19

are yellow and orange flowers bursting from behind one-foot arched lettering that spells out DeVries Nursery.

Dot must have noticed us gawking because she says, "Pretty attention-grabbing, huh? Dad did it himself—can you believe it? He put in the windows and the hydraulic liftgate. Even painted it himself. Cool, huh?"

The rest of us tried to look sincere as we smiled and nodded. After all, who am I to criticize someone for going a little crazy with green paint? And the liftgate *was* cool. It powered up the plants and buckets of flowers in no time, so all we had to do was shove them up against the cab.

When we're done, Dot asks her dad, "You want us to ride in back and keep the buckets from spilling?"

He says, "Hmmm," then shakes his head. "I don't think that's such a good idea." He looks over his shoulder. "Where *are* those boys? How long can it take to find a length of rope?"

Dot gives him a secret grin. "It's Stan and Troy, Dad—it can take all day!" He grins back and shakes his head, so she adds, "It's probably not even a mile, and you do need something to keep these from sliding around or tipping over."

Marissa and I shrug and say, "We don't mind. It'll be fun!" and Holly adds, "And then we can help you unload them, too."

Mr. DeVries laughs and says, "Okay, then. What can happen in a mile, *ja*?"

We all laugh and say, "Right!"

Ha!

THREE

We bumped along Meadow Lane and made it back onto the main road without spilling a drop. Mr. DeVries checked on us a couple times through the cab's pass-through window, calling, "You girls all right back there?"

And we were rumbling along fine, taking the curves in the road with no problem, when all of a sudden Mr. DeVries slams on the brakes and swerves.

It's amazing what a little swerve can do to you if you're in the back of a delivery truck. There's nothing to hold on to because *everything*'s slipping and sliding around, so you just kind of go with it. And even though we managed to keep the plants and buckets from falling over, that didn't stop *us* from taking a tumble. I landed sideways on my shoulder holding up a bucket of flowers, and so did Holly. Somehow Dot and Marissa stayed upright, but Dot's pant leg got soaked.

Mr. DeVries calls, "You girls all right?"

One at a time, we say, "Yeah...!" and then Dot adds, "What's wrong, Dad? What happened?" but Mr. DeVries is already outside, slamming the driver-side door closed. And since we couldn't see much out front, we rolled up the back door and scrambled out.

The truck wasn't exactly parked, it was just stopped in

the middle of the road. So we ran over to the shoulder, and that's when we saw her—the Lady in Black.

She had on a black dress with a black wool coat over it, and shoes that looked like black army boots, only with buckles instead of laces. A small black purse was looped around her arm, and arching across her white hair was a fuzzy black hat with a little black feather sticking out of it—like a Robin Hood cap, only velvet. She was frail, and hunched over so much that she'd have to get way up on her tiptoes to reach the five-foot mark.

And it was strange enough, seeing this crooked old woman decked out in boots and all black, but ambling alongside her was a pig. A big black pig with a big black satin bow attached to its collar.

Mr. DeVries gets in step beside her. "Ma'am! You're blocking the road!"

She stops walking, then cocks her head to look at him. "Blocking it? Young man, that's quite an exaggeration. You have plenty of room to go around."

Just then a silver Town Car with tinted windows rounds the bend toward us and slows down. And even though we can't really see the driver, you know he's in there wondering what in the world a bright green truck, a black-bowed pig, and a four-foot woman are doing decorating the roadway.

Mr. DeVries waves the car along, then tries to coax the Lady in Black to the side of the road, asking her, "Are you lost?"

She gives him a coy little smile. "Hardly."

"Are you on your way somewhere?"

"That I am."

"Would you like a lift?"

She eyes him. "I'm afraid that wouldn't be proper."

By now we've moved so that we can practically reach out and touch her, but she hasn't seemed to notice us.

Holly asks, "Is that a *pet?*"

The Lady in Black doesn't jump or act startled, she just turns and smiles like she's known we were there all along. "Hmm. A pet. No, I'd say Penny is more like a friend."

Then she turns to look at me, and it's the strangest thing. Even though her skin is wrinkled and so thin that her cheekbones seem ready to poke right through, her eyes are clear. Clear and bright, and very blue. And suddenly she doesn't look like your average old woman out for a walk with a big black pig. She may be tiny and have a weak voice, but in her eyes there's something very strong about her.

She grins down at Holly, who's petting her pig. "Like animals, do you?"

Holly smiles. "Yes, ma'am."

Mr. DeVries holds his hands out like he's talking to God. "In the middle of the road? Girls, I'm trying to get her to the side!"

"No cause for panic, young man. I'll move aside and you can be on your way."

He scratches his neck and says, "Are you sure we can't give you a lift?"

"That's very kind, but as I said, it wouldn't be proper."

Marissa says, "Well, where are you headed?"

"Just up the road a piece."

23

Dot asks, "You wouldn't be going to the Murdock party, would you?"

"I don't know that I would call it a *party*."

Mr. DeVries asks, "But is that where you're headed?"

She nods.

"That's where we're headed. Why don't you let us give you a..."

She looks him square in the eye. "And you are...?"

Dot says, "Oh, I get it!" She takes a step forward. "This is my father, Jan DeVries. My name's Margaret— but everyone calls me Dot—and these are my friends Marissa, Holly, and Sammy. We're on our way over to the Murdocks' to deliver some plants and flowers. My father runs a nursery—we just moved in down Meadow Lane."

She looks at us one at a time, then nods and smiles. "Pleased to make your acquaintances. I'm Lucinda Huntley." She turns to Mr. DeVries. "If you're sure you've got the room?"

Mr. DeVries looks completely confused.

"Now that I've made your acquaintance...?"

"Oh! Oh, certainly." He moves to open the passenger-side door. "There's room for you up front, but your pig will have to ride in back."

Lucinda corrects him, saying, "Her name's Penny. And if it's all the same to you, we'll both sit in back with the girls."

"But ma'am, there're no seats back there."

"That's all right. Just mind the curves." She smiles. "And pedestrians. Can't have you swerving to miss something you should've been expecting."

Mr. DeVries is figuring out in a hurry that there's really no arguing with a four-foot woman in a Robin Hood cap walking a two-hundred-pound pig, so he bites his tongue and liftgates both of them into the back.

The rest of us scramble in, then anchor the plants and buckets while Mr. DeVries gets back in the cab and throws the truck in gear. Lucinda Huntley makes Penny sit beside her, then sizes up the situation. "A length of rope would've done the job nicely."

Dot laughs. "My brothers are still out looking for one."

Lucinda winks at her. "Brothers can be like that."

"Besides, Dad had to get these to the Murdocks right away, and it's not far."

Her eyes sharpen on Dot. "Are you friends?"

"With the Murdocks?"

She nods.

"No, ma'am."

"The name's Lucinda."

Dot blinks at her a bit, and you can tell she's thinking that anyone so old can't possibly have a name without a Mrs. or Miss attached to it and that maybe she'll just get around the whole situation by not calling her anything at all.

Lucinda's onto her. "Say it."

"Excuse me?"

"My name. Go on, say it."

"Uh…Lucinda."

"Good. Now you were telling me that you are *not* friends with the Murdocks, is that right?"

"They just placed this order with my dad for their party, that's all."

Lucinda nods, then asks, "Are you going in?"

"To the house? Probably, but just to help unload."

She adjusts her Robin Hood hat, then looks around at all of us. "Good."

I can tell she's thinking something, and that something has nothing to do with stealing from the rich and giving to the poor. So I ask her, "Why do you care if we're going in?"

Penny snorts and nudges her, so she gives her ear a rubbing and says, "It'll just make things easier."

"How's that?"

She cocks her head my way and gives me a closed smile. "Sammy, is it? That would be short for Samantha?"

"Uh…uh-huh."

"And are you always so inquisitive, Samantha?"

"I wasn't trying to be inquisitive…I was just wondering, that's all."

"Hmmm," she says, like she doesn't quite believe me.

The truck slows way down and then turns up a driveway. Lucinda looks at me and whispers, "I just don't want trouble."

"Trouble?"

"Trouble," she says, but her blue eyes are twinkling.

What I wanted to ask her was, How do you expect me *not* to ask questions when you say something like that? but the truck was slowing to a stop, and I could tell from the way she was fixing the bow on her pig that the subject was closed. Instead, I peeked out one of the vent windows and asked, "You really think they're going to let a pig in that place?"

She muttered, "I don't see why not…*they've* been living there for years." Then she looks out the window and her jaw drops. "Land sakes! Are you sure this is the Murdock place?" She scoots across the truck to the opposite window and says, "There's the oak…and the wagon wheel…" She moves back to look at the house. "Lord! Have they taken on airs!" She straightens her hat again and says, "Well, airs or no airs, I'm here, I'm dressed, and I'm goin' in!" She gives Penny a nuzzle, then says to Holly, "You'll take care of her, won't you, dear?"

Holly says, "Sure," and before you know it, Penny's down and off on a walk with Holly while the rest of us tag along with Mr. DeVries to the front door.

Now, if I'd been thinking, I'd have realized that we weren't delivering flowers to a New Year's party. I mean, Lucinda had said something about it not being a party, but she'd been walking two hundred pounds of pork in the middle of the road, so I'd just figured she had a few pickets missing in her little white fence. But after talking to her in the back of the truck, I should have known that the things she said were connected. Definitely connected.

Mr. DeVries rings the bell, and right away the butler answers the door. He's wearing white gloves and a bow tie, and his eyelids are at half-mast as he says, "Yes?" down his nose at us, but it's hard to take him seriously because planted smack-dab on the tip of his nose is the biggest, reddest, ripest zit I've ever seen. It's like a volcano, ready to erupt.

The Volcano decides that it would be best for the Murdocks' white carpet if Mr. DeVries, who's a little bit muddy, and Dot, who's a little bit soggy, carry the plants to the foyer while Marissa and I shuttle them from there into the parlor.

So we get to work. And I'm carrying a tall ficus plant, not even thinking about Lucinda, who's like my shadow, shuffling alongside me, when we turn into the parlor. And *that's* when I finally make the connection. And I practically drop my ficus, because down an aisle between rows of padded white folding chairs is a casket. A shiny mahogany casket draped in an enormous cascade of white flowers.

Marissa's eyes bug way out, and she whispers, "It's a *funeral?*"

Lucinda claps her hands lightly and says, "Oh good. He's here."

I look at her and ask, "Who is it?"

"Johnny James Murdock."

The Walking Volcano stands to the side of the casket and snaps, "Over here with those." Then he points and says, "Group them all right here. Miss Murdock wants to place them herself later."

Marissa and I deliver our plants, then follow the Volcano around the casket and back up the aisle to the hallway. And when we get to the foyer where Mr. DeVries and Dot are dropping off the next group of plants, I bug my eyes at Dot and whisper, "It's a funeral!"

"What do you mean?"

"This party...it's a funeral!"

"You're kidding!"

The Volcano just stands at attention, twitching his nose like there's sulfur in the air. "You know the way," he says to us, then waves Dot off to follow her father for the next load.

Marissa and I take our plants down to the parlor, but when we turn in to the room I practically drop my load *again,* because the mountain of flowers on the casket has been pushed way to the side.

And there's Lucinda, standing on a chair by the casket, wrestling open the lid.

FOUR

I rush up to Lucinda and say through my teeth, "What are you *doing?*"

"I didn't come all this way not to have a few words with him," she says, then turns back to the casket. "Give me a hand, won't you?"

Now, I'm not about to help her pop open a casket so she can have a chat with some dead guy, but before I can tell her so, she's done the job herself. She steadies the lid, then gets down from the chair and stands by the casket, looking inside like she's sneaking a peek at a baby in a bassinet. She eyes me. "A moment of privacy, if you please."

I don't know *what* to do. I pull a face at Marissa, who's standing guard at the doorway, and she kicks into hyper-dance. But since Lucinda's staring me down, I back off and watch while she has her little conversation with a corpse.

Finally, she turns to me and says, "Certainly doesn't look like a murderer, does he, Sammy?"

I take a few steps closer. "A *murderer?*"

She nods, then leans in for a better look. "They did a nice job getting him ready. Normally you don't see so much color in the cheeks."

Well, he didn't look too rosy to me. He looked dead.

Very old, and very dead. And since I hadn't actually seen anyone inside a casket before, I didn't feel up to analyzing the mortuary's makeup job. I backed away and asked, "Who'd he kill?"

She gives me a little smile. "Someone very special to me."

"So why in the world are you *here*?"

She pats her purse. "I was invited."

All of a sudden Marissa comes hurrying into the room whispering, "Someone's coming! Quick! Close it! Somebody's coming!"

Very calmly, Lucinda looks back into the coffin and says, "It's funny. I was expecting to feel something, but I don't. This might as well be a stranger."

I'm about to reach up and close the casket myself, but there's no time. A large woman in a black dress and pearls has already come into the room.

At first, she doesn't notice that anything's wrong, so Marissa and I just put down our plants and head back up the aisle for another load. But then it dawns on her that the casket is sitting there wide open.

She stops in her tracks, and when we try to go around her she pops her hands on her hips, and there we are, stuck at a human dead end.

"What is going on here?" she demands.

"Uh...going on?" We shrug and say, "We're just bringing in the plants you ordered."

"That casket didn't fly open all by its lonesome, girls." She considers Lucinda for a nanosecond, then crosses her arms and glares at us. "What is this? Morbid curiosity?

How *dare* you?" Then she hollers, "Ma! Ma, get in here!"

Lucinda shuffles up the aisle and says, "Now hold on there."

"Ma! Ma-*a!*"

It seemed weird hearing a woman who had to be at least forty crying for her mother, but she kept right on squawking like a chick in a nest until her mother appeared in the doorway.

"What in heaven's name is the matter, Dorene?"

Dorene puts her hands on her hips. "Look what these girls have done!"

Lucinda shakes her head and says, "I've been trying to tell you, the girls had nothing to do with it."

"They…well, then who did?"

Lucinda gives her a little shrug.

"You?"

She nods and says, "I'm sorry I didn't have the chance to reposition things. If you'd like I can—"

Dorene says, "No! Don't you touch it!" and runs down to do it herself.

Lucinda says, "Well then, I'd best be on my way." She shuffles up the aisle past Marissa and me, and it looks like she's going to do-si-do out the door, but Ma blocks her path, saying, "Now wait just a minute. Who *are* you?"

Lucinda gives a slight shake of the head. "I'll just be going."

Their eyes lock for a moment, and then the mother's jaw drops. "Oh my god."

Dorene says, "What, Ma? What?"

"It's Lucinda."

"Lucinda?"

"Lucinda Huntley."

Dorene's eyes bug out, and she pops a pudgy hand over her mouth. "No!"

"Now don't get your panties in a bunch," Lucinda says, then snaps open her purse and produces a letter. "I've got an invitation."

Ma's face is like stone. "Impossible."

"See for yourself."

Ma takes the letter and reads. And I can see from where I'm standing that this is not your average time-place-date kind of party invite. It's a full page, handwritten.

Midway through, Ma's jaw drops. "He *apologized*?"

Lucinda nods. "It's a nice gesture, anyway."

"A nice gesture? It's insane! How could he *ever* apologize to you?"

"I can see that the story that's been passed along to you doesn't exactly paint things in the proper light, but regardless, he didn't do it with much time left, now did he?"

Ma looks at the upper right-hand corner of the paper. "Why, it's dated the twenty-eighth. That's the day he died…!"

"So I couldn't exactly come for coffee."

"Coffee?"

Lucinda taps near the bottom of the letter. "Right there. I came today instead, and we had our little talk. I trust he heard me." She opens her purse again and says, "Under the circumstances I think it would be proper for

33

me to return this." She puts a gold pocket watch into Ma's hand and takes back the letter.

"What is that, Ma?" Dorene practically rips the watch out of her mother's hand. "MVM...who's that?"

Ma's eyes are locked on Lucinda. "Manny Vernon Murdock."

Lucinda snaps her purse closed and says, "And now I'll be going." She steps around them and heads down the hallway.

"Wait a minute!" Ma chases after her. "You have a lot of nerve, returning this watch after all these years!"

Lucinda stops and cocks her head up at her. "Would you prefer I kept it?"

Ma sputters for a minute, then says, "No! I'd prefer if you'd stay off our property."

Lucinda gives her a hint of a smile. "Advice the Murdock clan should've taken years ago. Could've saved a lot of heartache."

"Don't you start up with me about that! If you think for one minute you can come in here and place blame on us for the misery you Huntleys have caused..."

Lucinda scowls at her and mutters, "There's no doubting you're a Murdock."

"What was that? You come back here. What was that you said?"

Lucinda shakes her head. "I'll be on my way."

"You'd best be! We don't need the likes of you ruining our funeral!"

Dorene steps up beside her mother and calls, "Yeah! You think you can do this and get away with it? Wait until

34

I tell my uncle what you've done! Lord knows you'll burn for this!"

While all this shouting is going on, poor Dot and her dad are standing on the porch with a bunch of plants, looking like they just stepped onto a minefield. I whisper to Dot, "I'm going to get her out of here."

"What *happened?*"

I shake my head. "That's a very good question." I check over my shoulder and add, "I'll meet you back at your house."

Dot nods. "You know the way, don't you?"

"Just back down the road to Meadow Lane, right?"

"See you there."

I guide Lucinda past the DeVries' truck, down the drive, past the wagon wheel and the old bent oak, and when we get to the road, there's Holly, walking the pig.

Holly waves and calls, "Hey!" and as we get closer, she says, "Penny is so smart!"

Lucinda smiles. "That she is."

I say, "We're walking back, you want to come?"

"You're *walking* back?"

I roll my eyes.

"What happened?"

"Well, let's see. The party's a funeral. Lucinda here decided to open the coffin and have a chat with the dead guy. She got caught. We got thrown out. You know—just a run-of-the-mill delivery."

"Oh, it wasn't *that* bad." Lucinda squats down to give Penny a kiss between the eyes. "I'd say they were almost civilized. For Murdocks, anyway."

Holly's still processing. "You opened the *coffin*?"

Lucinda shrugs. "There are some things one should say face to face."

I caught her eye with mine. "And you had something to say to him about him killing someone uh...special to you?"

Her head bobs a bit. "Among other things."

Holly's eyes open a stage further. "Wait a minute...are you saying the dead guy's a murderer?"

Lucinda reties Penny's bow, then stands with a sigh. "It's a very long story."

I look straight at her and say, "We've got a pretty long walk ahead of us."

She grins at me. "Not long enough, my dear. This story is generations old."

But she starts walking, and as soon as we're in line beside her, she starts talking. "The Murdock clan came over on the same wagon train as my great-grandma Huntley. Her name was Mary, and she had a little boy, Ezekiel, who was ten."

Holly says, "So wait, they were pioneers?"

"That's right. Now at the time, women didn't just join wagon trains without a man, but Mary had lost hers to typhoid. She had nothing but bad memories holding her back, and all those stories of the New Frontier creating an itch to go. So she planned it all out. She spent some savings on a wagon and supplies, cut her hair short, and fashioned a moustache from the clippings. Then she dressed herself as a man and joined up with an emigration party in Independence, Missouri."

"No one knew?" Holly asked.

"Not a soul."

"So what happened?"

"She managed to keep her identity secret for all of five days. The party was being ferried across the Kansas River by Indians when one of *them* spotted the deception."

"One of the Indians?"

"That's right. And it created such consternation among the Indians that they almost turned on the emigrants."

"Why?"

"It's unclear in the diary, but I believe they thought Mary was an evil spirit."

"So she took the moustache off?"

Lucinda laughed. "One Lewis K. Murdock *ripped* it off."

"And that's what caused the trouble?"

"That was only the beginning. Lewis Murdock didn't take kindly to the deception and mounted a campaign to have Mary banned from the wagon train. But Mary told the others that, woman or not, she could and would do the work of two men, and since Ezekiel had already proven himself to be a worthy hand, the party was convinced not to turn them back.

"Unfortunately, from that day forward the emigrants were plagued by misfortune. Hailstorms, wayward oxen, attacks by unfriendly Indians, broken wagons...and as the bad luck continued, more and more they blamed it on Mary. Moustache Mary they called her, and worked themselves into believing she'd cursed their journey.

"Then, with supplies diminishing and winter approaching, the families started turning on each other. Stealing from each other. Mary was one of the few with flour left in her barrel, and she found there was someone among them who had no compunctions about dipping in for their own needs.

"So she assembled the emigrants and made the announcement that she needed what little flour she had left for her boy, who was skin over bones and still working twice as hard as any other lad on the train, and that the next one who stole from her would be adding a bullet to the flour in his belly." Lucinda stops for a minute to catch her breath. When she starts walking again, she says, "Which is how Lewis K. Murdock met his demise."

"She caught him?" Holly asked.

"Red-handed."

"And she *shot* him?"

"As promised."

Holly and I look at each other and say, "Wow," and Holly adds, "Welcome to the Wild West!"

Lucinda nods. "Things were different then, and sometimes, I think, more honest. But for Mary, that's when the real trouble began. You see, Lewis was traveling with his brother, John, and John had with him his wife, Theodosia, and their boy, James. And since James was near grown and as spiteful as his father, Mary lived in fear that she and Ezekiel were more likely to die by the hand of a Murdock than that of an Indian."

"But Mary and Ezekiel did make it over, right?" Holly asked.

"Oh, to be sure. But as fate would have it, they staked out a parcel here, and the Murdocks staked out one—well, you saw it—right up the hill."

Holly said, "But why so close to each other?"

"The Murdocks didn't intend to stay. That was common knowledge. John just wanted to avenge his brother's death—or at least make sure Mary did not prosper—and then move on."

"So what happened?"

"Cholera happened."

"Cholera?"

"People used to die of it all the time. It's a nasty business. Your intestines turn on you. Retch you inside out. It did John Murdock in."

I thought a minute and said, "So that left Theodosia and James neighbors with Mary and Ezekiel. Two widows and their sons."

She smiled at me. "Just so. But the similarities in their situations didn't bring the women to an understanding. Theodosia fueled in James the notion that Mary was a curse, and Ezekiel grew up believing that somehow, somewhere, a Murdock was going to get him. Probably in the back."

"And?"

"And as it turns out, the Murdocks prospered, and so did the Huntleys. And the feud might have died out entirely if a certain descendant by the name of Johnny James Murdock hadn't been so easy with a trigger."

Holly asks, "So who's Johnny James?"

I hitch a thumb back up the hill. "The old guy in the coffin."

Lucinda gives me a little scowl, but she doesn't say anything. Instead, she points out the wire fencing that starts at a ravine and runs from post to post along the road. "This marks Huntley property. It's been over sixty years since a Murdock's crossed the line, and until I received that letter a few days ago, I thought I'd go to my grave without ever setting foot on Murdock soil again."

"So what happened?" I ask. "How was Johnny James easy with a trigger?"

All of a sudden Lucinda stops. "Well, look at this," she says, pointing to a gap in the bottom of the fence. "This isn't the proper way to mend a fence."

At the gap, there's a four-by-four post, cemented solid into the ground. But the section that meets it is damaged, and isn't long enough to be nailed in place. Instead, it's tacked around a smaller post, which has been connected to the top of the four-by-four with a leather strap.

Lucinda goes up to the fence, and while she's trying to work the two sections closer together, she says, "Johnny James was easy with a trigger in that he'd shoot at people without thinking things through."

"People? As in more than one?"

Lucinda keeps tugging on the fence. "Oh, sure. Not that he'd hit what he was gunning for. He was too hot-headed to be accurate."

"But he did hit someone?"

"In the end? Oh, yes."

"Well…? Who?"

She inhales deeply, hesitates, then says, "His own brother."

Our eyes bug out. "His brother!"

"Like I said, he was too hot-headed to be accurate."

I shake my head and ask, "Well, who was he *trying* to shoot?"

Lucinda stands there a moment with her hands on her hips and a scowl on her face. Then she eyes us and says, "Me."

Suddenly the smaller post falls, pulling its section of fencing inward. *"You?"*

She gives us a closed smile as Penny steps through the break in the fence and snorts at us from the other side. "Me," she says, then turns her attention to the fence again. "I'm going to have to tell my nephew about this." She gives us a mischievous little grin and says, "But let's follow Penny, shall we? It'll be a shortcut to the main house, and I can show you Mary's cabin."

We stood at the fence for a minute, watching her shuffle toward a grove of oak trees. And I knew I couldn't just let her disappear without finding out what in the world had happened with Johnny James Murdock and his brother, and one look at Holly told me that she couldn't, either.

So we step through the fence and put the sections together as best we can, fastening them with the strap of leather.

Then we're off, chasing after a little old woman, her black-bowed pig, and one Wild West story.

FIVE

Penny seemed to know just where she was going. And when she turned to check for us, her curly tail flipped clear around, practically wagging her whole rear end. We caught up to Lucinda and asked, "So…?"

She looks us over. "So?"

"So why would Johnny James want to kill you?"

Lucinda sighs. "Understand that between the Huntleys and the Murdocks there was a line drawn. We'd been taught early on not to cross it, and I never gave much thought to it. That's just the way it was.

"Then one year some folks in town decided to get together and put on a dance. It was a huge affair. People from clear up and down the state went, and of course I did, too.

"And it just so happens that the boy I danced the night away with was Johnny James' brother, Manny Murdock."

"Didn't you know it was him?"

Lucinda laughed and shook her head. "I hadn't seen him since his pa came to the schoolhouse one day all worked up about something and collected Manny and Johnny James. After that they worked full-time for him. Manny was about nine, I was seven, and Johnny James was quite a bit older, maybe twelve."

"How old were you at the dance?"

"Seventeen years, two days."

"Well, didn't someone introduce you?"

"No, we met at the pie table. He was after the last piece of rhubarb cobbler, and so was I. We decided to cut it in two, and after that he asked me to dance. He was a marvelous dancer, and so funny! I found myself laughing like I'd never laughed before, and by the time we went outside for some fresh air, we were both completely smitten."

"And that's when he told you his name?"

"As fate would have it, a friend of his brother's came over and said, 'Evenin', Manny. Is Johnny James here tonight?'"

Holly put a hand in front of her mouth. "What did you *do*?"

"I was speechless. And after the other fella left, Manny turns to me and says, 'What's wrong? You look like you've seen a ghost.' I just stared at him and whispered, 'You're Manny Murdock?' He makes some apology about not having introduced himself properly, then asks me for my name.

"So I told him. And we both stood there for a moment with our mouths gaping open, and then we started laughing. Just howling. He made some joke about my not having a moustache, and I said something about him not stealing my piece of rhubarb cobbler, and we just couldn't stop making jokes. None of the stories I'd heard about the Murdock clan seemed to matter—all I could see was Manny."

"What did your parents say when they found out?"

"Oh, Pa was mighty upset and did his best to talk me out of him, and I in turn told him Manny shouldn't be condemned for the sins of his ancestors. But Manny's family was like a nest of hornets. They tried everything. They lectured him, they threatened him, they dragged him down to the cemetery and made him apologize to every ancestor that ever died. They told him I'd be a curse on his life, just as Mary had been a curse on Lewis and John. And when shoveling all that guilt around didn't work, they'd lock him up in his room for days, hoping he'd come to his senses. And when he didn't, they'd turn around and give him extra duties to make up for the time he'd lost *not* coming to his senses. Finally, Johnny James figured there was only one solution: Get rid of me."

"So he came gunning for you?"

"That's right. He was brave with liquor and came right onto this property. Right over there. Just this side of that rock."

We look to where she's pointing, and what we see is a rock about the size of a refrigerator that's got yellow-and-brown moss growing on it and is sunk at an angle into the ground. And all around it is brown grass and oak leaves—not exactly a spot I would have pictured for a showdown.

"Manny and I were out for a stroll. It was a lovely evening, and he had just given me his pocket watch. I was admiring it, asking him if he was sure he wanted me to have something his pa had given him, when suddenly he jumped forward and shouted, 'Johnny, no!' The next thing I knew, there was Johnny James aiming at me from behind the rock, and Manny was flying in front of me with his arms spread wide. He caught the bullet, right in his heart."

The three of us stand there for a minute, silent, looking at Showdown Rock. Finally, Lucinda lets out a sigh and says, "As much as I lost that day, Johnny James lost more. I can see that now from his letter. He's carried the burden of his actions all these years." She gives Penny a quick ruffle behind the ears, then smiles at us and points down the path. "Mary's house is this way if you want to see it."

On the left there's Showdown Rock and a group of oak trees that are looking pretty bent and decrepit—like the wind could puff them right over if it was in the mood to. But on the right are rows and rows of reddish brown plants strung up on wires. Lucinda says, "This is our vineyard. The plants look like scarecrows this time of year, but in the spring it's a lovely sight. Green as far as the eye can see. The fall harvest was down again, but I'm sure Kevin will find a solution to that."

I ask her, "Kevin?"

"My nephew. He manages the vineyard. A harder-working man has never lived."

We walk along until we come to a little building on the edge of the vineyard that looks like a cross between a guard shack and an outhouse. Lucinda mutters something and starts hiking toward it, but suddenly the door swings open and a guy in dirty blue jeans and muddy work boots steps out. And he would've looked filthy from head to toe if it hadn't been for his *head*. It was squeaky clean. He had shiny straight hair the color of honey and bright brown eyes, and there wasn't a whisker on his face. And around his neck was a puka shell necklace with a one-inch tusk like a shark tooth hanging from the middle. He looked like one of those pictures where they take different people and piece them together. You know, Surfer Sam's head on the body of Freddy Farmer.

Anyway, when the door swings open, he jumps back a little and so does Lucinda. Lucinda says, "Dallas! You startled me."

"Afternoon, Miss Lucinda," he says, then leans down and gives Penny a friendly pat on the side. "What brings you clear out here?"

"I was on my way to show these girls the cabin when I noticed the toolshed door wasn't shut tight."

Dallas reaches into the shed, pulls a chain to switch off the light, then closes the door and snaps the padlock. "Going to lock me in, were you?" He grins and says, "That'd be a nice way to start the New Year—locked inside a toolshed."

Lucinda blushes. "I wouldn't have done that. But why *are* you here today? I thought Kevin gave you the day off."

"He did, but I had a few things to finish up, and then...well, you know how it is—there's always work to do."

She gave him a stern look. "Exactly. Which is why you need to take time off when it's offered."

"Just trying to turn our luck around. Besides, working a little extra is the least I can do after the way you and Kevin took a chance on me." He chuckles and says, "I can't exactly afford to *lose* this job, and if next season's anything like the last one, that's probably what'll happen."

"Nonsense. You'll have a job as long as you want it, and since you have no control over the weather, fretting about next season's crop isn't going to do you an iota of good."

He eyes us and says, "So who are your friends?"

"These young ladies helped me home from the Murdocks'. This is Samantha, and this is Holly."

He sticks out his hand. "Dallas Coleman."

"Dallas is our foreman. He oversees the crew, and I don't know what we'd do without him."

Dallas laughs. "This time of year I'm the foreman *and* the crew." He points in the direction we'd been heading. "So, these girls know the history?"

"Most of it."

I look to where Dallas is pointing and do a double take. I mean, the whole time we'd been standing around I hadn't noticed that less than thirty feet away, under the arm of an ancient oak, was what had to be Moustache Mary's cabin.

As we got closer, I couldn't help thinking that the Big Bad Wolf wouldn't have had to huff and puff very much to blow *this* cabin over. The sideboards were weathered and warped so badly that sunshine streaked through them like they were branches of a tree, and what roof slats were left were so mounded with oak-leaf mulch that the roof looked like a gopher racetrack.

Holly and I circled around it, and when we got to the door, Lucinda said, "Come on in, take a look."

We stood near the doorway, but when Lucinda insisted,

"Come in, come *in,* it's not going to bite," Holly and I stepped inside while Dallas kept Penny company outside.

I've always thought that living at Grams' was tight. Confining. I mean, if there weren't walls in the way to stop you, you could hose the whole apartment down with the kitchen-sink sprayer. But as I stood there in Mary's cabin, Grams' apartment was starting to seem roomy. For one thing, there were no walls to hose down—there wasn't even a kitchen sink. For another, the roof was really low; I could almost reach up and touch it.

On one side of the room was a stone fireplace with its chimney poking straight through the roof. On the other side were a few grape crates tossed around, a flat-edge shovel, and a rusted old hoe. And in between was nothing but a dirt floor covered in mulch.

As I walked around inside, two things struck me: One, it smelled vaguely weird. Not like dirt or old wood or mulch, more like sweaty gym socks. And two, despite the condition of the planks, I could see traces of blue paint on the walls. I asked Lucinda, "Huntley isn't a *Dutch* name, is it?"

She says, "No…what makes you ask?"

"It looks like the walls…and the *ceiling* used to be blue."

"That they were. It helped with the bugs."

"The bugs?"

Lucinda nodded. "That's right. Bugs don't like blue. They won't light."

"Really?"

She nodded again. "They didn't have the luxury of screening then."

Holly says, "I guess this is what Mr. Holgartner means when he talks about one-room cabins in history." She points to the arched fireplace. "This was for cooking?"

"And heat. They used to prepare meals here, eat at a small table right about there, and sleep across the room. Of course, the roof kept out the rain, and the walls were intact."

I'm shaking my head. "But still…"

Lucinda grins. "Not exactly the lap of luxury." We're all silent for a moment; then Lucinda says, "Shh! Shh…did you hear?"

Holly and I stand stock-still, listening. We both look at her like, Hear what?

She holds up a finger. "There! Did you hear her?"

Since Lucinda had said, "Did you hear *her*?" I knew right away that there was only one person she could mean: Mary. And she was looking so intense, with one crooked finger in the air and her blue eyes so wide open, that I held my breath and listened, too. Hard.

And what did I hear? Not a thing. Just the wind rustling the oaks outside.

Lucinda let out a deep sigh; then her face seemed to wash with a peaceful, faraway smile. "This is why I can't let Kevin tear the place down. I've told him her spirit's still here, but he doesn't feel it like I do. Dallas has heard her voice, but Kevin…I think he's afraid to. He seems to block her out."

We listen for another minute before Lucinda says, "Let's go see her, shall we?" and shuffles out the door.

Holly and I back our way outside and practically trip

over Penny, who's rooting around at the base of the cabin. Dallas grabs her by the collar, and I whisper to him, "Have you really heard Moustache Mary's voice?"

He looks real serious and nods. "More than once. She has a very strong presence here. And you might want to leave off the Moustache..." He looks around cautiously, like someone might be listening. "Around here, anyway."

We join Lucinda, who's standing a few feet from a stone grave marker, which reads MARY ROSE HUNTLEY, BELOVED MOTHER. "My father had her moved to the Stowell Cemetery to be with Ezekiel and the rest of the family, but I believe her soul didn't go with her remains. I believe she's still right here."

Holly asks, "Why's there still a headstone here?"

"Father got a new one. Fancier. I prefer the original myself. I had no say in the move, mind you, but I've always disagreed with it. Once you're laid to rest, you should be allowed to rest, not dug up and moved across town."

Dallas says, "You're right about that, Miss Lucinda. I sure wouldn't want someone moving me around."

"Precisely."

Penny shakes free from Dallas and heads back to the cabin. Lucinda says, "She'll be fine, Dallas," but he follows her anyway.

Lucinda studies the tombstone a minute, then turns to us and whispers, "I've seen her. I'm sure of it." She points across the vineyard to a faded yellow clapboard house in the distance. "From my window. Kevin thinks my eyesight's going"—she frowns—"or my mind, but I know what I know, and I know what I've seen."

Holly whispers, "What did it look like?"

Lucinda turns her blue eyes up to study Holly, and when she's sure she's not making fun of her, she looks back at the tombstone and says, "Not a ghost like you see on television—more a glow in the air. I've never gotten very close; she's always vanished before I could get down here, but it's definitely not my imagination."

Well, I wasn't about to stand around Moustache Mary's old grave and ask a bunch of questions about ghosts. I mean, ghosts rank right up there with werewolves and vampires—if they *do* exist, I'm going to get as far away from them as I can, as fast as I can, and for once I'm not going to ask one single solitary question.

So we're standing next to Lucinda, looking at the tombstone, and I'm thinking it's time to get out of there, when I hear a twig snap, right behind us. I whip around and so does Holly, but Lucinda doesn't even blink. She keeps her eyes on the ground and says, "Hello, Kevin."

Kevin's big. Tall and big. And for a guy who didn't actually cross the plains in a wagon train, he's sure looking like he did. He's got on a pair of baggy blue jeans, tied up with a length of thick rope, some cowboy boots and a cowboy hat, a flannel shirt, and a tattered scarf around his neck. And everything he's wearing looks sun-bleached and dusty. Even *he* looks worn out—like he's walked for days across the desert without sleeping.

Lucinda smiles at him and says, "Kevin, I'd like you to meet my new friends, Holly and Samantha—they walked me home from the Murdocks' today. Girls, this is my nephew, Kevin Huntley."

He barely looks at us. "You actually went there?"

"It wasn't so bad. I feel better for having cleaned that slate."

He shakes his head. "They must've thought you were crazy."

"I don't much care what they thought. As far as I'm concerned, it's over."

Kevin scowls, then notices Dallas holding Penny by the collar. He looks confused for a second, then says, "Didn't I give you the day off?"

Dallas nods. "I wanted to catch up on a few things."

"It'll keep. You should go enjoy the day." He tips his hat without even looking at us and says, "Nice to meet you," then heads off through the vineyard.

Lucinda sighs as she watches him go. "I'm suddenly weary."

Dallas coaxes Penny along until she's beside Lucinda. "You want me to walk you up to the house?"

"That'd be nice. Girls, you should come this way, too. It's shorter for you to go back to the road out the front drive."

So Dallas and Penny walk beside Lucinda while we follow, a few steps behind. And when we get to the Huntleys' house, it's easy to see that it's plenty big—it's got two stories with lots of windows and a big, shady porch—but it looks as worn and tired as Kevin. The yellow paint is faded and peeling, and the roof seems to sag under the weight of the sky.

When Lucinda steps onto the porch, Dallas rubs the tusk on his necklace and says, "You know, I should probably stick around and help Kevin. He shouldn't give me the day off if he's not going to take it himself."

Lucinda scolds, "No. Just because he's forgotten how to enjoy life doesn't mean you should. Go!"

Dallas laughs, then gives her a playful salute and hops off the porch with a "Yes, ma'am!" He turns to us. "Which way are you guys headed?"

Holly says, "Down to Meadow Lane."

"Let me give you a ride on my motorcycle. We'll all fit, and we ought to let Lucinda get some rest, okay?"

We shrug and say, "Sure," then wave good-bye to Lucinda. But as we're walking away, I glance over my shoulder, and there she is, looking small and frail on her broad, sagging porch. And I get this chill and an eerie vision of the house collapsing all around her—swallowing her up.

SIX

It's not like it was *that* far back to Dot's, and really, we probably wouldn't have taken a lift from Dallas if he hadn't insisted. But there we were, crammed onto the back of his motorcycle, me straddling big metal saddle-bags, holding on to Holly, and Holly in the middle, hanging on to Dallas. It reminded me a lot of getting a ride from Marissa.

Dallas comes putting to a stop at the end of the Huntley driveway, and while he's waiting for a pickup truck to go rumbling by, he flicks away a few oak leaves that have wedged themselves between cables by the speedometer and says, "She's a neat old lady, isn't she?"

We both call, "Yeah," and he calls back, "Too bad no one ever found that gold. Could've made all the difference."

Holly says, "What gold?"

He checks us out in his rearview mirror, then rubs it clean with the sleeve of his shirt. "I thought she told you the story!"

"She didn't tell us about any gold!"

He pulls out onto the main road and shouts, "Maybe she's given up. When I first came on, she had me digging holes all over that property. There's some crazy riddle in

Mary's diary about rocks and ridges and hidden treasure, but *I* sure haven't been able to help her out."

I shout, "You've seen the diary?"

"What?"

I shout louder, "Have you seen the diary?"

"Oh, sure. Ask her. She'll show it to you."

Now I've got a million questions colliding in my brain, but it's kind of hard to ask questions in a sixty-mile-an-hour windstorm when you're hanging on for dear life. So I just hunker down, and before you know it, we're squeaking to a stop at Meadow Lane.

We peel ourselves off the bike and try to sound grateful when we say, "Thanks!" And I was planning to ask him some questions about the gold, but then I notice that Holly's looking kind of green. Besides, Dallas doesn't give me the chance. He flashes us a smile, calls, "See ya!" and then kicks up dust getting back on the road.

The second he's gone, Holly fans the air in front of her and makes a choking sound. "Oh my god."

"What?"

"I need a bath. Oh, yuck!"

"What do you mean?"

She's still fanning air. "Didn't you *smell* that?"

"No…"

"Oh God, you are so lucky. I can't believe you couldn't smell him."

"Dallas?"

"Yes, Dallas! That guy has the worst B.O. I have *ever* smelled, and believe me, I've been around some pretty rank people."

I guess I was looking pretty surprised because Holly fans the air one last time, then heads down Meadow Lane, saying, "Next time you ride in the middle. Oh, pew!"

So much had happened since we'd left Dot's house that you'd think Holly and I would be jabbering about Moustache Mary and Lucinda and what Dallas had said about some stash of missing gold, but we weren't. We just walked along, doing some mental sorting. Then, when we get to the DeVrieses' porch, Holly asks, "Do you think they should've moved her?"

Right away, I know she's talking about Mary. "To the cemetery downtown?"

"Uh-huh."

"I don't know."

"Well, do you think she's still there?"

I look at Holly. "I guess it depends on whether or not you believe in ghosts."

Dot throws the door open and says, "Why are you guys just standing there? Come on in!" She practically drags us in, then shuts the door behind us. "What took you so long? We were starting to think you got lost."

Now this is not a question you can answer in one word, or even one sentence, so I guess it's a good thing Dot forgot she had asked it in the first place. She heads off, saying, "C'mon! We've got to set up the carriage house before it gets dark. Marissa's out there putting up the cots. Can you help me with these sleeping bags and pillows?" Then she loads us both down with flannel bedrolls and leads us outside.

Their carriage house is actually really neat. It's like a

barn, only without hay or horse poop. Not that there isn't the *potential* to have fresh and processed hay—there are two stables with a loft over the top—but both are empty and the room smells more like bleach than organic oats.

Marissa sees us and says, "Oh, *now* you show up. I've pinched about every one of my fingers."

Marissa's not what you'd call a mechanically minded individual, so I probably should've known better, but I flopped onto one of the cots and right away, *snap! snap!* I'm trapped in a tangle of springs and aluminum.

It might have only hurt, except the place that got hit the worst was my arm—right where I'd scraped it on the asphalt—so it *killed*.

Marissa comes running over and does the McKenze dance, trying to figure out how to untangle me. She pulls down one end, but it snaps back before I can get out. Dot rushes over to help her, and Holly pulls down the other end, and I roll out.

Marissa squats beside me and says, "Sammy, I'm so sorry! Are you all right? I guess I forgot to push the locks down on that one."

I hold my arm and glare at her, so she says, "Sammy, I'm *sorry*. It was an accident. Sammy, stop it! What else do you want me to say?"

I mutter, "How about 'Timber!'?" then force up a little grin.

At first she doesn't get it, but when Dot and Holly laugh, she remembers my little adventure on her handlebars. She says, "Oh, Sammy. I'm so sorry!"

The throbbing in my arm's starting to go away a bit, so I stand up and say, "Yeah, right. I know what's really going on: Heather's hired you to kill me, hasn't she?"

Marissa's eyes pop wide open. "Sammy!"

"Why else would you catapult me through the air and feed me to a man-eating cot?"

She's looking really worried, like she's not sure if I'm kidding or not. So I grin and say, "Marissa, it's all right. I'm fine."

"Are you sure?"

I hobble around like I've just come home from a war. "Oh, yeah. Never felt better."

She throws a pillow at me. "Stop that!"

"Ooooo! Getting serious now. We've advanced to pillow warfare!" I hurl it back at her. "Well, take that, you turncoat!"

She throws it at me again but hits Holly instead, and pretty soon the four of us are flinging pillows and sleeping bags and just basically pounding on each other. Finally, I get a sleeping bag over Marissa's head and roll her around, and after a minute of struggling to break free, she cries, "Surrender! I surrender!"

So I set Marissa free from her flannel prison, and we're all sprawled out on the floor laughing when we hear someone snicker.

We look over at the door, and standing there are two boys, older than us, but not much. The taller one's got a paper bag choked in one hand. He says, "Wow. Nice party," and the other chimes in with, "Yeah. Looks like one of Bep and Anneke's."

Dot snaps, "If you can't be nice, just mind your own business, all right?"

They take that as an invitation to come in. The taller one asks, "So who are your friends?"

Dot scowls at him, but then mutters, "Holly, Marissa, Sammy, meet my brothers, Stan and Troy."

We all make little waving motions while we size each other up, then Stan chokes down his paper sack a bit more and gives us a little scowl. "I can't believe you're actually gonna sleep out here. I guess you're braver than I thought, Dot. *I* sure wouldn't sleep out here. Not with"—he waves a hand through the air—"you know."

Dot hesitates, then shakes her head. "What are you talking about?"

Stan looks at all of us like, Uh-oh, and heads for the door. "Uh...never mind. I'm sure you'll sleep fine."

"Stan!" Dot grabs his sleeve. "Quit trying to spook us!"

His voice drops and he says to Dot, "Sorry. Forget I said anything. I didn't know you didn't know."

Dot's face crinkles up. "About *what?*"

He looks her straight in the eye and whispers, "About what happened in here."

"*What* happened in here?"

"Some lady got trampled by a horse." He looks up at the rafters. "Apparently she's still here."

She lets go of his sleeve. "Oh, shut up! You're trying to tell us this place is haunted?"

"It's true. Ask anyone in the neighborhood." He laughs. "Or just tell me about it in the morning."

He and Troy head for the door, but you can tell Dot doesn't want him to leave yet. And you know she's dying to ask him more about the ghost, but she stops herself and instead she asks, "Uh…what's in the bag?"

He holds it up a bit. "Oh, this? Just some entertainment for tonight."

"Like what kind of entertainment?"

He pulls out a string of firecrackers. "American entertainment."

Troy grins and says, "We even got bottle rockets."

"Dad's going to let you do that here?"

Stan scowls. "Are you kidding? We're on our way to Pioneer Village. Marko says the block parties over there get better every year."

"What about *sjoelbak*? Aren't you going to play?"

He laughs. "Like I said, we're gonna have some *American* entertainment."

They leave, and when Dot turns around, the look on her face is confused, almost sad.

Holly asks, "What's the matter?"

Dot sits down on a cot—which stays together just fine—and says, "We've always played *sjoelbak*. The whole family. And usually I wish Stan would just disappear 'cause he's such a pain in the neck, and he gets Troy acting all high and mighty, too. But now that he *is* going away…" She shakes her head. "I don't know. It's just weird."

Holly tries to cheer her up with, "Well, it's not like there aren't going to be enough people…*we're* going to play, right?"

Marissa says, "Yeah. Where is this *sjoelbak* thing, anyway?"

Dot jumps to her feet. "Oh, that's right! We never did find it. Let's clean this place up and go check the basement."

We pick everything up and tidy the cots, then follow Dot back toward the house.

The DeVrieses' basement wasn't through a skinny door and down some creaky stairs. Its entrance was outside, and the door was lying flat on the ground. Dot pulls up the door and we all stand around, looking down into this big black hole.

Marissa balks. "We're going down *there?*"

Dot laughs and says, "It's not spooky once I get the light on. Wait here if you want. I'll go down and turn it on."

She disappears into the darkness, and after a minute the light comes on and she calls, "Come on down!"

So we file down the stairs, and the temperature drops with every step we take. The walls of the basement are plaster with big chunks missing, and the ceiling is only about seven feet high. There's a water heater, a furnace, and a bunch of pipes overhead, and then a group of pallets keeping boxes off the cement floor.

Holly says, "Wow, this is cool!"

Marissa rubs her arms and shivers. "Literally."

Just then the basement ceiling creaks and we all look up. Dot says, "We're under the kitchen. That's Mom walking around up there."

I say, "Listen! You can hear her talking!"

Dot says, "Yeah. There's a cupboard in the kitchen that has vents from the basement. In the old days they used the cupboard for storing potatoes and stuff you wanted to

61

keep cool. Dad says he's going to board it over, but so far he hasn't."

Marissa says, "Well, I'm freezing! Is that thing down here or not?"

Dot laughs and says, "Let me check back here." She climbs behind the boxes and a minute later she calls, "Here it is!" and a six-foot plank of rosewood with a one-inch curb on three sides comes scooting over the boxes. "Can you reach this?"

Holly grabs one end and I grab the other, and when Dot reappears she yanks on the light chain and says, "Let's go."

We hauled the *sjoelbak* up and out, and then Dot and I carried it like a stretcher into the house. We propped it against a wall near the dining room table and then wandered into the kitchen, where Dot's mom was draining water from a pan of boiled potatoes.

Dot says, "We found the *sjoelbak*, Mom."

"Great, hon." She puts the pan down. "Maybe you could set the table? Only for eight. The boys are spending the night at Marko's." She takes one look at Marissa and says, "Do I need to turn the heat up?"

Marissa laughs and then chatters, "No, I think I'll just go get something warmer on."

So while the rest of us work at putting blue-and-white dishes on a bright blue tablecloth in the middle of a half-blue room, Marissa runs out to the carriage house to get a sweater. And we've just set out little windmill salt shakers when Marissa comes stumbling back inside.

She's not wearing a sweater or a jacket, and she's still looking about as warm as an ice cube, only now her face has got about as much color, too. I say, "Marissa, are you all right?"

She nods, but her eyes are fixed straight ahead. Finally, she whispers, "But I think I want to go home."

Mrs. DeVries comes over and eases her into a chair. "Are you sick?"

Marissa shakes her head.

"Then what is it? You look like you've seen a ghost."

Marissa turns to Mrs. DeVries and whispers, "I don't know what else it could've been."

SEVEN

Marissa looked like she'd seen a ghost all right, but I just couldn't buy it. I kneeled down next to her chair and said, "Marissa, there is no ghost. You just got spooked going out there by yourself."

She snickers. That's all—just snickers. So I stand up and say, "Okay, so tell us what you saw."

"Go see for yourself if you don't believe me."

So we all go traipsing outside, me up front like I know exactly what I'm *not* going to see, and Mrs. DeVries in the back, coaxing Marissa along. And when I push open the carriage house door, I don't see white or light or anything ghoulish—what I see is a mess. There are clothes hanging from the rafters, others flung around the floor, and one of the cots is jackknifed closed.

Marissa looks straight at me. "See? And you should've heard the sound!"

"What sound?"

"It was a...a *ghost* sound!"

Now maybe if I'd been out there in the middle of the night by myself, I would've been spooked, too. But I wasn't out there by myself, and it wasn't even finished getting dark yet, so it was easy to say, "Marissa...this wasn't done by a ghost! Stan and Troy probably did it to try and scare us."

Dot walks around with her head back, looking up at the rafters. "But Stan and Troy left half an hour ago!"

"That doesn't mean they didn't come back…"

Off in the distance a bell is ringing. Mrs. DeVries says, "That's our phone. Are you girls going to be all right?"

We say sure, so off she goes, and the minute she's gone Dot says, "If Stan and Troy did this, I'm going to kill them."

We start picking clothes up and pulling them down, and Marissa's just starting to get some color back in her face when we hear, *Woooooooo… Wooooooooooooooo!*

Marissa gulps, "There! Do you hear that?"

Everybody freezes, and there it comes again, *Woooooooo… Wooooooooooooo!* Marissa screams and runs out the door, then stands outside looking in at the rest of us, rooted like plants in a pot.

Dot whispers, "Where'd that come from?"

I point one direction, Holly points the other.

Dot looks at our arms shooting off in opposite directions and doesn't go anywhere. And we stand there for another minute, waiting for the sound to come again, and that's when I notice that the fog's coming in and it's gotten dark outside. Not pitch-black, but definitely dark.

Marissa whispers from the doorway, "Get *out* of there!"

*Wooooo… Wooooooooooo…*comes the sound again, and then on top of that comes a moaning sound—like someone far away, in a lot of pain.

We uprooted, all right, and we might have just bolted into the house if Dot hadn't grabbed us outside the carriage house and said, "Wait!"

We stare at her. "For *what?*"

She looks me in the eye. "Do you believe in ghosts?"

"No."

She turns to Holly. "Do you?"

Holly shrugs.

"Marissa?"

Marissa shifts into hyper-dance. "I do now!"

Dot shakes her head and says, "This is stupid. C'mon," then turns around and marches back into the carriage house.

Now what am I supposed to do, let her go into the Ghost Zone by herself? So I go charging after her, and the minute we're inside she points and says, "You look over there, I'll look over here."

Dot goes off in the direction of a stack of cardboard boxes, and I scoot my way over to a column of wooden pallets. But before I've had the chance to look behind the pallets, I hear Dot snap, "Get out of there. Get out now!"

A giggle floats through the air like a string of bubbles, and then Dot's got her little sister by the arm, demanding, "Where's Anneke?"

Beppie giggles some more, then points across the room to the stack of pallets. I look behind it and sure enough, there's the other ghost, looking like Little Miss Mischief.

She scrambles out and ducks around me, then escapes with her sister out the door and into the night.

Dot shakes her head and says, "Those two drive me bonkers." By now Holly and Marissa have come inside, so she says to the three of us, "Look, why don't you guys go back in the house. I'll clean this mess up."

We all say, No, no, we'll help, and before you know it, we've got the place picked up and put back together. And we're just about to close the door when Mrs. DeVries appears, wiping her hands on a dish towel. "There's a boy on the phone who says he wants to talk to Marissa."

"To *me?*" Marissa asks, pointing to herself. "Who is it?"

"He wouldn't say." She rubs crusted dough off a thumbnail with the towel. "I'm sure he's the one who called while I was out here, but the first time I picked up the phone and said DeVries he just hung up."

Marissa says, "I'm...I'm sorry about that," and then shakes her head. "I wonder who it could be?"

I whisper, "Mikey?" because being rude is what Marissa's little brother does best.

She shakes her head and shrugs, and then we all follow Mrs. DeVries into the house like ducklings back to the water.

Marissa picks up the phone and says, "This is Marissa," and then she just stands there, listening. After a minute she mouths something, but we can't understand it. Then she says into the receiver, "Sure she'll want it back. She's right here, do you want to talk to her?" She looks straight at me, but when I ask, "Who is it?" she holds up a finger, telling me to wait. Then she says into the phone, "I don't think we can do that...no, we're celebrating New Year's at our friend's house." She's quiet for a long time and then turns her back on us because we're bugging her so much, trying to find out who she's talking to. Finally, she motions for a pencil and says, "Okay, I'll take it down and

I'll ask them. Maybe we will, but I can't say for sure." She writes some stuff down, then gets off the phone and says, "Guess who that was." Like we hadn't spent the last few minutes trying to do just that.

"Who?"

"Taylor."

"Taylor?"

"Uh-huh. And guess why he was calling."

I roll my eyes and say, "I don't even want to know."

She laughs. "Sure you do. His friend wants to give you your skateboard back."

"Snake? Seriously?"

Marissa says, "He called him Jake, but yeah, the guy you plowed down."

I almost said, That *I* plowed down? but instead I scowled and said, "Jake-the-Snake. Good name."

"Whatever. They're having some kind of New Year's Eve party at Taylor's house over in Pioneer Village, and he says he wants us to come bury the hatchet."

"*Taylor* does?"

"That's what he said…"

I sat there for a minute, thinking. I mean, maybe Snake-face had developed a conscience, but from what I knew of Taylor there had to be more to this than my skateboard. I look Marissa up and down and say, "You know what's going on here, don't you?"

"What do you mean? He says his friend scraped off the paint and could see something had been written under it so—"

"No, what's *really* going on here."

"What do you mean?"

"I mean with Taylor."

Marissa just stands there looking completely confused.

"He likes you."

"What?"

"Taylor *likes* you."

"Oh, stop!" She blushes, then looks to the others for help.

Holly shrugs and says, "I'd say that's probably pretty accurate."

Dot's already on beyond who-likes-who. "How'd he get this number?"

Marissa sits down and kind of mumbles, "He called my cousin, Brandon, who called my mom…" She looks up. "I don't think he *likes* me. I think he just wants to give back the skateboard."

I let out a snicker.

"What?"

"Really, Marissa, come on. Why didn't Jake-the-Snake call *me*? And why does Taylor want you to go to his party? Why doesn't one of them bring the skateboard here?"

"I don't know…maybe he's just trying to be nice. Besides, he didn't invite *me*, he invited *us*."

"Oh, right. Like he wants a fourth grader at his New Year's party."

"Sammy, you've got to get over that!"

"Think about it, Marissa."

She looks down and says, "Quit it, okay? *I* don't want to go over there…I just thought you might want your skateboard back."

Dot says, "Did you say it was in Pioneer Village?"

Marissa nods.

"That's where Stan and Troy went. They have block parties over there. I've heard they last all night."

I look at her. "So what are you saying?"

Dot shrugs. "We could go there later if you want."

"I don't *want* to go to Taylor's party. I want to stay here, and if ol' Snaky wants to return my skateboard, he knows how to find me."

The three of them look at me like I'm selling snail slime. Holly asks, "Why are you so mad, anyway? I thought you really wanted that skateboard back."

Dot says, "Yeah, you practically killed that guy this morning trying to get it away from him."

I sat there for a minute with my arms crossed and my bottom lip out. Finally, I said, "It just feels wrong."

Holly shrugs and says, "Well, it's your skateboard—you tell us if you want to go get it."

Mrs. DeVries says, "In the meantime, let's have dinner."

So we put the finishing touches on the table, and before you know it, Mr. DeVries says, *"Smakelijk eten,"* which apparently is Dutch for "Dig in."

I guess I didn't know how hungry I was, because before Beppie and Anneke had the pea eyes pushed into the potato men they were building, I was looking around for seconds.

Mr. DeVries eyes me and says to Dot, "That one's a good eater." Then he points his fork at Holly and says, "That one, too."

Holly and I look at each other and kind of blush,

but then Holly says, "Well, we missed lunch 'cause of Lucinda."

Dot's mom says, "You should've said something!"

Mr. DeVries laughs. "I think they're making up for it now, *ja*?" Then he shakes his head. "That old woman was very strange. I thought the Murdocks were going to throw me out on my ear. What was she *doing* in there today?"

So Holly and I tell him. About Lucinda opening up the coffin so she could make her peace with Johnny James face to face, and then about the Huntleys and the Murdocks coming west in a wagon train; about Moustache Mary shooting a Murdock; about the Murdocks homesteading up the road from the Huntleys and all the trouble that came from that. And when we get to the part where Johnny James winds up shooting his own brother, Mrs. DeVries puts her fork down and says, "That's horrible!"

Then we tell them about Showdown Rock and seeing Mary's cabin and what it was like. And Holly and I are like relay racers—she tells part, then I take over and tell the next part, then hand the story back off to her. And we're both running so hard at the mouth telling them all about what happened that we don't even realize we're heading straight for the part about Moustache Mary's ghost until we're there. All of a sudden we both clam up and look at each other like, Oops!

There's no going back, though, so we sputter up again. And pretty soon we're running full throttle, telling them about ghosts and lights and Mary's grave site.

When we hit the finish line, Marissa says, "Oh, great.

First it's a ghost in the carriage house, now it's that Mary woman. This whole place is zooming with ghosts!"

Dot laughs, "Yeah, and two of them are sitting right here."

Beppie and Anneke giggle and you can tell—their haunting days are far from over. Mrs. DeVries eyes them and says, "You're asking for an early bedtime, *ja*?"

They both button their lips and shake their heads like little angels.

Dot rolls her eyes, then sighs and says, "Can we have some *oliebollen* now?"

Mrs. DeVries pushes away from the table, "Sure, sweetie. Let's get the dishes cleared first."

So we all help clean up, and when the place is spic-and-span, we sit back down at the table to a platter of *oliebollen*. Dot and her sisters dive right in, but Holly, Marissa, and I inspect ours pretty good before we try them. They're about the size of tennis balls, only they've got crunchy strands of batter and black things that look like coffee beans poking out of them—like little caffeine grenades that someone's tried to camouflage with powdered sugar.

The tip of Dot's nose is dusted with sugar, but she doesn't know, or doesn't care. She takes another bite and says, "Try one!"

Marissa points to one of the black things. "What are these?"

Dot takes another *oliebol* off the plate. "Raisins."

"*Raisins?*"

Mrs. DeVries says, "They lose their wrinkles when you fry them."

The three of us pull faces at each other like, Oh, yum.

Mr. DeVries laughs. "You girls like donuts, right? These are our New Year's donuts. Try one."

So we take a bite. And another. And another. And pretty soon we're dusted cheek to chin in sugar, too.

When we're all good and stuffed, Mr. DeVries sets up the *sjoelbak,* and we take turns trying to slide and slam these two-inch wooden pucks into slots at the end of the board. And even though I'd never played shuffleboard of any kind before, I had a great time being only a few points behind Dot on the chase to high score.

But then suddenly I hear something through the clatter. Something in the distance. And at first it almost sounds like a television on somewhere in a back room, but when I'm sure it's not, I say, "Shh! Listen!"

The room quiets down, and sure enough, there it is— sirens. After a minute Mr. DeVries says, "I wonder what that's about."

Mrs. DeVries says, "I hope nobody's hurt..." She turns to Dot, and you can see the worry in her eyes. "Do you think Stan and Troy—"

Dot stops her before she can finish thinking it. "They're fine, Mom."

"I have Marko's number, but...I'm not sure about the house. Do you know where he lives?"

"In Pioneer Village. Mom, you're—"

"But *where* in Pioneer Village?"

"Mom, if you're that worried, just call!"

I look at them and say, "Well, it's not an ambulance."

Mrs. DeVries asks, "How do you know?"

"Listen."

So we all listen again, and after a few seconds I say, "There! Hear that horn? That's a fire truck."

Mrs. DeVries looks a bit relieved, but as much as I try to tell myself I'm being silly, I've got this uneasy feeling that those fire trucks haven't come clear out to Sisquane to douse some fireworks.

No, something's happened—something terrible.

EIGHT

There was no answer at Marko's house and you could tell—Mrs. DeVries was still worried. So Dot asks us, "You guys want to ride over to Pioneer Village? It's only about five minutes up the main road. We could try to find Stan and Troy and then go get Sammy's skateboard."

Everyone else was up for it, so I said, "Sure," and after we promised Mrs. DeVries we'd be careful, off we went.

Now Pioneer Village may have been only five minutes up the main road, but getting to the main road seemed to take forever. We couldn't see much because the fog had settled in, the light on Hudson's bike only worked well when I got up to a certain speed, and the potholes made going fast impossible.

When we finally got to the main road, we were planning to turn right, up the hill to Pioneer Village, but there was a car coming from the left and a truck with its lights flashing coming down the hill from the right. And as they approached Meadow Lane, I could see that the truck was a fire department Blazer and the car was a police car.

I guess they noticed that about each other, too, because they both slowed down and came to a stop, right in the middle of the road, about twenty feet from us. They rolled their windows down, and the minute they started talking to each other, fog or no fog, light or no light, I knew exactly who was driving that squad car.

I whisper to Marissa, "Recognize that voice?"

She nods and says, "You want to hide?"

I shrug and say, "Nah. We're okay."

"You and Officer *Borsch*? Since when have you two been 'okay'?"

Until that minute, I hadn't really thought that Officer Borsch and I *were* "okay." I mean, I have such a long, bad history with the man that I never really thought it was possible. But then I found out about his partner getting killed, and he finally figured out that I wasn't the juvenile delinquent he thought I was, and I don't know—it's not like we're *cured* or anything. It's more like we're in remission.

Dot cuts in with, "Listen! They're talking about a fire!"

Sure enough, Officer Borsch is saying, "We're just lucky they got those oaks out in time. This whole area would've gone up in smoke."

"Have they found a cause?"

"The investigators are looking now. Maybe sparklers, 'crackers, who knows? It was kindling waiting to light."

"Is the structure all cooked out?"

"Completely. There's a stone fireplace left, that's about it."

"I heard them radio for a paramedic—someone hurt?"

"Just an old lady in hysterics. You can go see for yourself, but I've got to get back. I'm slightly out of my jurisdiction."

The guy in the Blazer laughs, "What else is new, Gil?"

I couldn't stop myself. I called, "Are you talking about the Huntley cabin?"

They heard me, but over the sound of their engines, they didn't hear me very well. Officer Borsch turns off his motor but leaves his lights on, and I can see him looking around for where the sound came from. So I call again, "Are you talking about the Huntley cabin?"

He motions the guy in the fire truck to shut off his engine, and then there they are, parked in the middle of the street looking around for who's asking the question. I roll forward a few feet so I'm out of the shadows, then I straddle the bike and wave once like I'm cleaning a window.

For a second there I think Officer Borsch forgot that we were "okay." Even with the light blinding me a little, I can see him lose a few shades—like *he's* seen a ghost.

Holly rolls out beside me, then Dot and Marissa do the same. And we're all lined up like we're ready for a rumble when Officer Borsch calls, "And what would you know about the Huntley cabin?"

"Not much, I just want to know if that's what you're talking about."

"It is, but *why* do you want to know?"

In my heart I knew that they'd been talking about Mary's cabin, but when Officer Borsch actually said it *was*, well, all of a sudden my stomach went queasy and I felt like I was going to lose my *oliebollen*.

Holly sees me turning green and calls, "Lucinda Huntley gave us a tour of the place today."

Officer Borsch calls, "How well do you know her?"

Holly shrugs. "Well enough to know she's gotta be really upset that the cabin's burned down."

I whisper to Holly, "We've got to go see her."

Holly nods, but Dot says, "What about my brothers? We're supposed to be looking for them."

"They're fine, Dot. The sirens were for the fire, not Pioneer Village. You can go there if you want, or we can go afterward, but right now I've got to see Lucinda."

Holly nods. "Me, too."

Marissa says, "What do you want to do, Dot?"

Dot thinks a minute, then calls to Officer Borsch, "Have there been any other…uh…incidents in this area?"

"What do you mean?"

"Uh…you know…anybody get hurt or anything?"

Officer Borsch says, "Noooo…," like he's not real sure he wants to let her in on this valuable piece of classified information. "Why do you ask?"

Dot says, "No reason," and then whispers to us, "Okay, let's go."

Officer Borsch calls, "Girls?"

We look at him and say, "Yes?"

"Stay out of it, okay? There are plenty of professional people there taking care of things. Your friend is going to be fine. She just needs a sedative."

I felt like saying, A *sedative*…you don't understand! But I knew that arguing with Officer Borsch would turn the "okay" into "go away!" So I nodded and said, "Thanks for the information, Officer Borsch. It's too bad about the cabin, but I guess there's nothing much we can do about it." Then I turn my bike around and head up the hill toward Pioneer Village, and the others are looking at me like, Are you feeling all right? but they follow along.

I guess I made life a little too easy on Officer Borsch, because he's not buying it. The Blazer takes off, but Officer Borsch follows along beside us in his squad car and calls out the passenger window, "So where you headed?"

"Up to Pioneer Village."

"Pioneer Village, huh? To a party?"

"Yeah."

He nods and you can see his little wheels turning. "I was headed that way myself. Some of those parties can get pretty out of hand."

I laugh and say, "Just don't tell anybody that we sent you!"

He laughs, too, then says, "Oh, and Sammy?"

"Yeah?"

"One last thing."

"What's that?"

"Keep back, okay? That's all I'm asking. Let the professionals do their job."

By now we've both stopped, and we're leaning over, looking at each other through the passenger window. I blink at him, and he stares at me. Then he says with a little smile, "You think I don't know you better than that?"

I straddle the bike, not knowing what to say. I mean, for the first time in my life I'm finding it really hard to lie to Officer Borsch. "You...you're not telling me I can't go?"

He laughs. "Experience tells me that that would be useless. Just keep back, and try not to *say* anything. The last thing they need are comments from the peanut gallery."

I nod, and before I can say thanks, off he goes to expand the detour from his jurisdiction, and we do a U-turn to expand ours.

We decided we'd have less chance of being stopped if we went past the Huntleys' driveway and entered through the break in the fence. So we rode along Lucinda's property, and pretty soon we could see lights flashing through the fog, and the smell of smoke became very strong. And the closer we got, the worse my stomach felt.

The break in the fence was easy to find. The whole section was slumped over. Holly looks at me and I look at her, and right away Dot asks, "What's the matter?"

So we tell them about the damaged fence and Lucinda being upset by it, and how we'd left it strapped closed. Marissa says, "So maybe some of the fire people came through here. Does it open up wide enough to drive through?"

That was a thought. We checked out the distance from one post to the next and decided that it was a bit too small to get a car through, and way too small for a fire truck.

Marissa says, "Maybe they drove up and walked."

"Maybe, but there's no one here now. They're all up the driveway, and *someone* came through this way!" Then it hit me that there might be tire tracks in the dirt. "Hey, you guys! Hold still! Don't move."

They freeze while I stoop down, trying to find tire tracks in the dark. Holly says, "What are you *doing*?"

"I thought maybe there'd be some tire tracks, but I can't see anything! I wish we had a flashlight."

Dot says, "Your bike's got a light. Too bad we can't just ride it in place."

I say, "Hey, that's it!" So I get Dot and Marissa to hold the back wheel off the ground while I grab a pedal and crank. As soon as it's going fast enough for the light to come on, we pivot the bike on its front wheel and scour the ground for tracks.

And what do we find? Just a bunch of footprints that the four of us had made.

Marissa croaks, "Sammy! Haven't we done this long enough? There's nothing to see!"

We stop and plop, and Holly says, "Well, if there was anything there, we messed it up walking on it."

Dot says, "I don't know why we're even doing this. I thought you guys wanted to go see Lucinda."

Everyone agrees that she's right. So we park our bikes inside, then close up the sections of fence, wrapping the leather over the post. Then we make our way toward the cabin, and as we pass by the toolshed, the smell of smoke becomes overwhelming. Nauseating.

Then, at the same time, we all stop and stare. The area is flooded with light glaring from the side of a fire truck, and poking through the ashes like a tombstone is the fireplace, charred and dripping water. And except for the fireplace, the cabin is gone. Completely gone.

There are a few firemen in rubber boots and hard hats talking to each other as they inspect an area off to the side with their flashlights. We stand there a moment, stunned, then Marissa says, "That was it?"

Holly and I nod, but we don't say a word. And I'm

feeling completely choked up about the whole thing, even though I'm telling myself that I'm being stupid. I mean, how long had I known Lucinda? Less than a day. And Moustache Mary was interesting, but she wasn't *my* ancestor. And the cabin? Well, really—it *was* just a shack.

So I'm standing there, trying to force the tears back into their ducts, when I get goosed.

That's right, goosed.

And I'm not talking just a little nudge in the behind, either. I'm talking full-on goosed. I squawk, and as I'm spinning around I see that what I've been goosed by is a pig. A big, black, bow-wrapped pig.

Penny's bow is half untied and looking pretty droopy, and no one would argue that she could use a bath in something besides mud. She snorts at me and then nudges me with her snout again, only this time she's polite enough to only offend my thigh.

With all the snorting and squawking we were doing, the firemen couldn't help but notice us. Two of them shine flashlights across the ruins at us, and even at that distance they're blinding. One of them calls, "We don't need any looky-loos here, girls. You'd better move along."

Then Dallas shows up. And if Holly thought he smelled before, he must've been completely ripe now. He was covered in soot, his shirt was torn and streaked with black, and his hair was dusted with ashes.

The firemen drop their lights and call to Dallas, "How's your grandmother holding up?"

Dallas seems dazed for a minute, looking at the rubble.

"She's not my—" Then he stops himself and says, "The doctors are with her."

One fireman asks, "She's not your grandmother?"

Dallas just keeps staring at the rubble.

The fireman takes a few steps closer and cocks his head a bit. "Then why'd you risk life and limb trying to put this fire out?"

Dallas closes his eyes and lets out a deep sigh. "Lucinda's been better to me than my own family. And this cabin meant the world to her." He looks the fireman straight in the eye and says, "So now what?"

"We've got the coals turned and the site's cool; it shouldn't be too much longer."

Dallas just nods. And when the fireman goes back to his group, I can't help it. I call, "That's *it*?" I take a few steps forward. "That's all you're going to do?"

Penny follows right beside me like a dog at heel, and then Marissa, Dot, and Holly come forward, too. I call over to the firefighters, "Aren't you going to investigate? I mean, the house didn't spontaneously combust. It got help. It got a lot of help!"

One of the firemen gives a little shrug and says, "Now, you don't know that."

"You think it started all by itself?"

"No, I…" He shakes his head, then lets out a sigh. "We see this sort of thing pretty regularly on holidays. This is the third one tonight alone. Kids sneakin' off to have a smoke, fireworks lit in an unsuitable environment, Satanic groups with some ritual gone wrong. It's not uncommon. My guess is, given the remoteness of the site, and the nature of the original structure, that's what happened here tonight."

"What do you mean, the nature of the original structure? That it was made out of wood?"

He picks up a spade that's leaning against the pumper truck and starts turning ashes over. "It was a shack. An old, abandoned shack."

"Maybe it didn't *look* like much, but this was the home of Mary Rose Huntley. A *pioneer*. It wasn't just a shack! It was a historical monument."

He stops flipping dirt and says, "A *monument?*"

"Well, it was important. To Lucinda, anyway."

"I understand. And I'm sure they'll send someone out in the morning to investigate further if that's what she wants."

Now while we've been arguing with the fire brigade, Dallas has been circling the ruins, holding the back of his neck, and kicking the ground from time to time. Like he's mad at the ashes.

When he gets back around to us, Holly asks him, "Can't you make them do something *now?*"

He keeps right on holding his neck, and his nostrils are flaring in and out as he breathes. "Oh, I want to, but what good would it do?"

Holly says, "What do you mean? You don't think some *kids* did this, do you?"

He looks at her like she's just interrupted a very complicated thought. "Investigating won't bring the cabin back. And frankly I don't think that this feud with the Murdocks will ever be over. Proving it was them would be like spitting into the wind."

Holly says, "The Murdocks? You think it was the Murdocks?"

"Lucinda does, and after hearing their comment about her burning for visiting them, I think she's probably right." He looks back at the rubble and says, "I'm going to go see how she's doing," then hurries off toward the house.

As we're watching him go, Penny nudges me in the thigh, first gently, then hard. And when I look down to scold her, she looks right at me and does it again, only this time she adds a great big snort.

There's no doubt about it—she's telling me to get a move on. So I say to the others, "You want to go see how Lucinda's doing?"

Holly says, "Yes!" and the others shrug and say, "Sure."

And as we head down the path to the main house, I look over my shoulder at the firemen turning the ashes of Mary's cabin. And it hits me that if the Murdocks really did burn the place down, no amount of turning coals is going to put that fire out. A little puff of wind would bring it right back to life.

Just as it had for over a hundred years.

NINE

They'd just given Lucinda a sedative when Kevin let us into the den. He said, "Try to keep it short. It's been a rough night," but the gruffness of his voice was oddly soft. Like he was too tired to turn us away and too upset to really want us not to be there.

Lucinda looked tiny, like a little girl, wrapped in a blanket on the couch. Dallas was sort of perched on the edge beside her, saying, "Lucinda, I've been thinking... Maybe I can rebuild it for you. The fireplace is still intact and—"

"Don't you do that to her!" Kevin steps out of the shadows of the hallway and says, "This is hard enough without talk like that."

Dallas stands up and whispers to Lucinda, "I'll come see you tomorrow." Then he motions our way and says, "Your new friends are here," and leaves the room.

Lucinda smiles at us, then puts out a hand, saying, "Come in, girls."

We scoot in, and since her hand is still out, I take it. Her fingers feel cold and hard. Like I'm holding a bouquet of bones.

When I sit down where Dallas had been, she looks at me sadly and says, "Where's she going to go?"

I know she's talking about Mary, and I can't think of anything comforting to say.

Holly whispers, "Maybe she's free now."

Lucinda looks at her. "Free…what a nice thought. Though I never considered the house to be her prison…" She squeezes my hand a little and says, "Would you bring me her diary? It's up in my room on the night table. Upstairs, last door on the left."

I look around to make sure it's okay with Kevin, but he's gone, so I say, "Sure," and head for the stairs.

The carpet on the steps is dirty and matted, and the flowered wallpaper has faded to a dusty yellow. And as I creak my way up the staircase, I feel like I'm surrounded by decay. Like I'm walking through the heart of a house that's dying.

I shake off the creeps and hurry down the hallway to the last room on the left, but when I open the door, the room feels the same as the hall and stairs had. The wallpaper's peeling and the ceiling has dark spots from water damage, and there are two places where the carpet's been seamed with duct tape.

I pull back the lace curtain of one of the windows to see if I can spot the cabin, and the cloth feels brittle, like if I pressed too hard, it would crumble in my hand. The fire truck floodlights are gone, and I can't see much through the fog, so I move over to the other window and there's Dallas out on the driveway with Kevin, and it looks like they're arguing. I try pulling up the window a little so that maybe I can hear what they're saying, but the thing's swollen shut and won't budge.

Then Dallas puts his hands up, shakes his head, and walks off, so I let the curtain down and get busy looking for the diary.

It's on the nightstand, all right, and I would've picked it right up and run downstairs if this framed photo of Kevin hadn't distracted me. In the picture a much younger Kevin is standing beside a truck loaded with grapes, and his face is bursting with happiness. I stared at it for a minute and couldn't help wondering—how long *had* it been since the Huntleys had had a good harvest?

I made myself put the picture down and pick up the diary. The cover was dark brown leather and the pages were thick. Heavy parchment thick. And except for a few blotches here and there, the writing was beautiful— curvy and flowing—not at all the kind of penmanship I was expecting from Moustache Mary.

The first page read simply: *Journal of Mary Rose Huntley*. I turned the page and the journal began:

April 10, 1845: It is with trepidation that I begin this journey. Ezekiel is but ten and has only of late learned the value of a secret well kept. I fear the repercussions, but fear more the regret of not having made the attempt. Our party left the encampment this morning, journeying away from Independence, Missouri, numbering but thirty-seven. Milton Kelsey, who is the company leader, assures us that this figure is ample, but I suspect that he was simply impatient, waiting for more to come up. It, at least, increases the likelihood that they will keep me, should I be discovered.

I wanted to read more, but made myself stop. I fanned through the diary once, listening to the pages crinkle against each other, then turned out the light and hurried back downstairs.

"Lucinda?" She was almost asleep when I sat down beside her on the couch. "Here you go. Here's the diary."

She smiled at me and whispered, "Thank you."

"I read the first page—I hope you don't mind."

"Not at all."

"It's...it's *amazing*. I didn't want to put it down."

She put the book in the crook of her arm like a teddy bear. "You can borrow the copy, if you'd like."

"The copy?"

"Kevin thinks this one should be zip-locked away somewhere. He made me a photocopy years ago. The words are all there, but I still prefer this one. Her spirit's in it." She motions across the room with her eyes. "Go on. The copy's on the bookshelf, right over there. See it? By the Bible."

Lucinda's words were slurring, and I could tell that she was fighting to keep her eyes open. So I found the copy of Mary's journal, and we whispered our good-byes, telling her again how sorry we were for what had happened. She nodded and then said, "Can you visit tomorrow? I'd like...," but she fell asleep before she could finish.

We tiptoed out of there and found Kevin on the porch, brooding. The band of sweat around his hat seemed to have crept up another half inch, and even in the cool, foggy air, he looked sweaty and dusty from head to toe.

He takes one look at us and says, "She sleeping?" When we nod, he lets out a sigh. "Best thing for her."

I held up the diary. "She said I could borrow this?"

"Go ahead," he says, and dismisses us with a wave.

As we're going down the steps, I look back at him and ask, "So what are you going to do?"

He shakes his head. "I'll discuss that with her in the morning."

Marissa tugs on my sleeve and whispers, "Let's go," so we hurried through the darkness to get our bikes.

We steered clear of the ruins because even from a distance the place gave us the creeps. But when we neared the fence, I got shivers anyway because the fence wasn't closed the way we'd left it. It was gaping open.

Dot whispers what we were all thinking: "Someone's been through here!"

Marissa says, "Can we please just get *out* of here?" but then Dot grabs my arm and says, "Look!" and points in the direction of the ruins.

At first, I say, "What?" but then I see it, faintly, through the fog—not a beam of light, more just a glow.

Marissa says, "What *is* that?" and Holly offers, "Maybe it's just someone with a flashlight out there."

But the more we watch it, the less it looks like someone walking or searching with a flashlight, and the more it looks like something none of us want to say.

Holly says, "Oh, come on. It can't be."

Marissa whispers, "Why not?" and Dot adds, "Yeah, why not?"

Holly says, "Well, for one thing, a ghost wouldn't have to open this fence. A ghost would float right through it."

"Yeah, and you know how things look weird in the fog," I say. "And they sound weird, too."

So we all agree that it can't be a ghost. But we don't all agree that we should go check out what it *is*. Marissa says, "Sammy, no!"

"Marissa, there are four of us. What could possibly happen?"

Holly says, "I'm game," and Dot says, "Me, too," but when we look at Marissa, she just stands there, doing the McKenze dance. So I say, "You can stay here and guard the bikes if you want…"

"By *myself*?"

I shrug. "If you want."

"Oh, all right," she groans. "I'll come with you."

So we sneak back toward the cabin, and while we're walking, we're whispering, "Do you see it?" "There it is!" "Look, it moved!" and stuff like that. Then, when we get to Showdown Rock, we hide behind it and just kind of hold our breath.

Now you've got to understand—whatever this is, I know it's not the ghost of Moustache Mary, Holly knows it's not the ghost of Moustache Mary, and so do Dot and Marissa. Well, at least Dot. But when you're standing in a place where someone's been shot dead and you're looking through the fog at something moving in the air, it's easy to become a believer.

And we're all completely petrified behind this rock when we hear a noise. A crunchy noise. A shuffly noise. A noise like someone—or some*thing*—walking through leaves.

Marissa whispers, "Do you hear that!?"

We all nod.

"What *is* that?"

Holly whispers, "It's not chains rattling, that's for sure."

I say, "Shhh. It's getting closer."

One look at Marissa and I know that, as much as she's trying to fight it, there's a scream working its way out of her body, and when it surfaces, houses all over Sisquane will be missing their windows. I cup my hand over her mouth and whisper, "Marissa, it's okay. Really, it's okay!"

But that sound is getting louder, and now, besides the crunch and shuffle, there's a low, guttural breathing sound. And it's not coming from miles away—it's right on the other side of Showdown Rock.

So we're all huddled up with our eyes as big as Frisbees, trying not to lose it, when what phantom being appears from around the rock?

One very dark, very big...pig.

It could've been a mouse. At that point it didn't matter. We screamed. I choked on mine, but Marissa's went straight through flesh and bone, and Holly and Dot rounded out the sound with some really shrill harmonics.

Penny didn't care. She just wagged her curly little tail and nudged around my feet like she was hunting for truffles. And after we got over the fact that we'd been sniffed out by a pig, we looked back at the cabin and knew—the ghost was gone.

We stood behind Showdown Rock for another few minutes, waiting for it to reappear, but it never did. Finally, Marissa says, "Can we *please* go now?"

Penny keeps rooting around, sniffing and snorting her way back toward the ruins. I say, "Why don't we follow Penny?"

Marissa rolls her eyes. "Oh, great. Now we've got a pig for a tour guide." Now it's not like Marissa to be sarcastic when she's scared. But she wasn't biting her nails or doing the McKenze dance, she was standing there with her hands on her hips.

So I laugh and say, "Boy, that scream did you a lot of good, didn't it?"

"What do you mean?"

I just laugh again and say, "Yeah, we've got a pig for a tour guide. Come on!"

Penny leads us over to the cabin, all right, and proceeds to nudge her nose through the ashes and chunks of timber while we circle the place. And it strikes me again how bad it smells and how *small* the place was. And all of a sudden I'm full of questions. Like, How do you raise a family in a place like this? How long did they live there? When did the other house get built? But mostly I kept coming back to: What's going to happen now? Would Kevin bulldoze the rest of it down? It did seem wrong. Very wrong. And what about Mary's old grave? Maybe her bones weren't there, but it did feel like her spirit still was.

And I found myself standing beside the ruins kind of overwhelmed by what had been. By the people who had built the place and lived their lives there. By the fact that they had done it day by day, with no electricity or running water, no trash collection or sewers, and all of a sudden I felt like a wimp, living at Grams' with a toilet and a refrigerator and a television.

And standing there by the ashes, I started feeling very strange—like something bigger than my thoughts was flowing through me—something I couldn't describe or touch, but could definitely *feel*. And it didn't give me the creeps as it tingled down my spine; I didn't want to scream or run, I just wanted to stand there and let it wash over me. Wash through me. It was like now I understood what this place meant—not just in my head, but in my heart.

Then I got goosed. By a pig, of course. And after I was done jumping, I turned around and said, "Stop that! Don't you *ever* do that again!"

So what's Penny do? She flips her tail and nudges me *again*.

"I said stop that!"

She takes this to mean, Nudge me harder.

I take a few steps back from her and say, "Quit it!"

Well, she scoots me along, step by step, until I'm away from the ruins and near the ravine. And when she's got me by the edge, she tries nudging me right over.

"Stop that, you crazy pig! What are you *doing*?"

Holly, Dot, and Marissa are following along, just cracking up while that stupid pig chases me in a circle, trying to get me to go into the ravine. And it's not that it's *that* steep—I just don't feel like being run down the hill by a pig. So I plant myself and say, "No! I'm not going! You hear me? I'm not some corn cob you can roll around. Stop it!"

She snorts at me, then goes in herself. And halfway down she turns back and oinks. Full-on oinks.

Holly says, "What is she *doing*?"

"I have no idea."

We're all standing on the edge, watching this hare-brained hog oink her head off, when I notice something. I lean over a little and point. "What is that?"

They all look, too. "What?"

"Right next to Penny. It looks kind of red."

"Where?"

It's half buried under some leaves, but I can see the corner of something shiny poking through. "Right there!" I scoot down the hill, and when I get beside Penny, I reach over and say, "What is that, girl? What have you found?"

Before I can touch it, she flips it up with her snout, and there, sitting in the leaves right in front of me, is a can.

A shiny new gas can.

TEN

For once I tried to be smart. I nudged the can with my foot, but I didn't touch it. And when I got down on my knees to sniff the thing, Marissa calls, "What are you doing? Sammy, what *is* that?"

"It's a gas can!"

Holly comes scooting down the hill. "A *gas* can?"

"Yeah, and I can smell gas on it."

Dot scoots down the hill after her. "You look like Penny, sniffing that thing!"

Marissa eases herself down the hill, too, and when we're all standing around the can, she says, "Are you going to take it to Officer Borsch?"

"No. For once I'm not even going to *touch* it. I don't want to mess up any fingerprints. C'mon. Let's go to the house and see if we can use the phone."

So we climb out of the ravine, then move a big white rock in a straight line up from the can to mark the spot. We call, "Penny! C'mon, girl!" and she trots alongside as we hurry back to the house. She follows us to the door, but then abandons us to eat vegetable parts from a giant metal dish over by her muddy bedding on the far end of the porch.

We try the bell, but no one comes. We try it again, only

this time I put my ear up to the door and listen for the sound. I can't hear anything, so I say, "Maybe it's broken."

So we knock. First kind of quietly, but since Lucinda's sedated and I'm sure Kevin's going to want to know about the gas can, it doesn't take long for us to start pounding.

The place is pretty dark. There's a light shining through the curtains of the kitchen, and one glowing from down the hall, but other than that, the house looks desolate.

Now none of us could imagine Kevin leaving or falling asleep so soon after what had happened, so we started banging again, only this time we also called out, "Kevin! Hey, Mr. Huntley! Please! Open the door!"

He didn't open the door, though. And no lights turned on or off. And we couldn't hear a thing from inside, only Penny, scarfing up scraps from her bowl.

Dot says, "Maybe he took a sedative, too. He seemed pretty upset."

Holly adds, "Why don't we just go back to Dot's and call the police from there?"

So we're tromping along, heading for our bikes, when Marissa says, "Wouldn't it be a lot easier if we just took the gas can to Dot's house? That way the police could get it from us there, and we wouldn't have to come back *here*."

She had a point. And when Holly says, "If you're worried about fingerprints, you could pull the sleeve of your sweatshirt over your hand or pick it up with a stick," and Dot chimes in with, "It's not like it's in its original location, either," I decide they're right. We'll take the can with us.

So we go back to the ravine, find the big white rock, and

I shinny down the hill, no problem. But then I can't find the can. Anywhere.

Marissa calls, "What's the matter?"

"It's not here." I hunt around some more and then look up the hill at them. "Is this the right spot?"

They check, then all three of them nod at me. Dot calls, "Are you *sure* it's not there?"

They wind up coming down the hill to help me search, but after a few minutes we stop, one by one, and look at each other. Holly whispers, "It's not here," and Dot adds, "Definitely not here."

Marissa says, "Which means that someone else *was*."

"Let's get out of here!"

I know they're right—that's exactly what we should do. But still, I'm having trouble giving up. I mean, without the evidence I'd have sub-zero credibility with Officer Borsch. Sure, for once I had some witnesses, but if I knew the Borsch-man, that would probably only make him four times as annoyed. Especially since I'd stuck my nose in when I'd told him I wouldn't.

But the rest of them were already scrambling out of the ravine, so I took one last dig through the leaves, then chased after them.

We got to the fence, pushed our bikes through, then wrestled the sections back together and blasted down the road. But when we got to Meadow Lane, they kept going straight.

I call, "Hey, wait! Where are you going?"

They stop, and Dot calls back, "I promised my mom, remember?"

"But…"

Marissa says, "You were going to call the police *now*?"

"Well, yeah…I thought…"

"Sammy! They're not even there to answer the phone. You'd have to call 911, and I hate to break it to you, but this is *not* an emergency."

"But…"

Holly says, "They're right, Sammy. The gas can's gone, so there's nothing to show them, and what can they do tonight, anyway? Let's just call them in the morning."

"But…"

They all three cry, "Sammy!" so I push off and grumble, "All right, all right…I'm coming."

When we turned in to Pioneer Village, it was clear that everything we'd heard was true—the place was Party Central. The yards and streets were swarming with people—kids, adults, teenagers—all kinds. And music was blaring from here and there, getting mixed up in the air as a happy-sounding noise.

Now to tell you the truth, I hadn't wanted to go to any Pioneer Village block party partly because it seemed kind of, well, scary. Like it would be dark and full of people I didn't know, doing things I didn't want to do.

This wasn't anything like that. There were sparklers going in the street, kids playing tag and keep-away, and adults sitting on lawn chairs with blankets covering their laps, just soaking it all in like they were at a parade.

Marissa says, "Wow! This is cool!" and then Dot spots her

brothers lighting off fireworks in the street with a couple of other boys. She points and says, "There they are!"

I figure she's going to want to go talk to them, so I head off in their direction, but she grabs me and says, "Sammy, stop! Where are you going?"

"Don't you want to talk to them?"

"Um...no. Let's just watch for a minute, okay?"

Well, I don't really understand this, but I back up and we all straddle our bikes and watch. After a few minutes, Dot whispers, "They don't even seem like Troy and Stan."

I look at her and ask, "What do you mean?"

"They seem different."

"*How* do they seem different?"

She shrugs and says, "I don't know...they seem... older. Especially Stan."

They seemed the same to me, but what did I know about brothers? Then this girl with short blond hair and big hoop earrings brings Stan a soda and nuzzles up to him.

Dot's mouth drops open. "Do you see that? That girl's putting moves on my *brother*."

We nod like, Yeah...we see it, but Dot's looking pained. *"Why?"*

I ask, "Why's she putting moves on your brother?"

"Yeah!" She shakes her head and says, "She must not know him very well..."

We laugh, and Marissa asks, "Why don't you go meet her?"

Dot rolls her eyes. "You trying to get me killed? No, let's just get out of here!"

But it's too late. Troy's spotted us and he's not wasting time in telling Stan who he's seen. You can practically hear Stan say, "What!?" and then he looks to where Troy's pointing—straight at us.

Stan whips his arm off Blondie and stands there looking really self-conscious for a few seconds, before he decides to come marching toward us. And by the time he gets to Dot, he's mad. "What do you think you're doing, spying on me?"

"I'm not spying on you...I'm...I'm..."

"Yes, you are!"

"No, really, we're here because...because we've been invited to a party."

"You're lying!"

"No, I'm not!" Then she looks down and says, "But would you call home and let Mom and Dad know you're all right? They've been trying to get ahold of you because of the sirens, but no one's picking up Marko's phone."

Stan says, "I knew it!" and is about to lay into Dot some more, but Marissa comes to her rescue. "Actually, Dot's not lying. We're on our way to a party at"—she pulls a piece of paper out of her back pocket and reads— "6324 Wagonwheel Road. Do you know where that is?"

"Wagonwheel's right around the corner." He looks at her kind of skeptically. "Whose party?"

Marissa says, "A guy named Taylor."

He blinks at her. "Briggs?"

Marissa nods.

He takes a step back and says to Dot, "No."

"What do you mean, No?"

"No sister of mine is going to a Briggs party."

"What!? How can you say that? Do you even *know* him?"

"I don't need to know him. I know Karl, and that's bad enough."

"Why? What's the matter with Karl?"

Stan shakes his head. "Just stay away from them, you hear me?"

"Stan!"

"I'm serious."

Dot says, "Actually, we're only going there to get Sammy's skateboard back."

"What's her skateboard got to do with it?"

I say, "It's a long story, but his friend's decided to have a conscience and give my skateboard back. We're just going to pick it up."

"Do you want me to go get it?"

We all say, "No!" I mean, that would be pretty embarrassing, sending Dot's brother to fetch my skateboard.

He looks straight at Dot and says, "Don't even go inside, you hear me?"

"All right, all right!"

He nods a little and says, "Okay," then heads off across the street.

Dot calls, "Don't forget to call Mom!"

"All right, all right!" he says, and goes back to his friends.

We head down the street slowly, going between sparklers and fizzers, and Marissa says, "What do you think that was about, Dot?"

"Oh, I don't know. He was probably just trying to spook us again."

Holly says, "He seemed pretty serious to me…"

Dot scowls and says, "Yeah, and how'd he seem when he was talking about ghosts in the carriage house?" She shakes her head. "Half the time I don't know *what* to think of him."

When we turned onto Wagonwheel Road, my stomach felt kind of topsy-turvy and I couldn't really figure out why. We found the house, then parked our bikes and went up the walkway, two by two.

There's a party happening inside, all right. The curtains are drawn, but we can hear music blaring. So I take a deep breath, reach out, and ring the bell. And after a couple of minutes of nobody answering, I reach up to push the button again, but before I can, the door flies open. And who's on the other side? Not Taylor or Karl. Not Baggy Boy or Snake.

No, it's the Vicious Viper herself—Heather Acosta.

ELEVEN

Heather looked like *she'd* just been goosed by a big black pig. And I'm afraid I probably wasn't looking too cool and collected myself because we both blurt out, "What are *you* doing here?"

The minute I asked I knew it was a stupid question. Taylor and Heather were friends. And standing there looking at her, I realized that they were a lot alike. Taylor was older and smoother, but you could tell that underneath was someone sneaky. Mean and sneaky.

So I put my jaw back in socket and said, "We're here to see Taylor."

She laughs, "Oh, *sure* you are," then comes in like a mosquito after blood. "Get out of here...all of you. There's no way you're crashing *this* party."

"We don't have to crash the party, Heather. Taylor invited us."

It was like throwing gasoline on a fire. Heather's face turns red, and she cries, "Liar!" then slams the door in my face.

We look at each other and bust up. Completely.

Now I wanted to be at this party about as much as Heather wanted me there. But I did want my skateboard back, and I had the feeling that if I didn't get it now, I might not get it back at all.

Marissa says, "Well, I don't think ringing the bell again is going to get us in—you want to go around back?"

We all look at her like, *Marissa?* because she's usually the *last* person to suggest going someplace we're not wanted.

She says, "Look, it's a party. Whenever my cousin has a party, people come in and out like they own the place." She perks an ear up. "I can hear people in the backyard—let's just go in the side gate and around that way."

If Marissa was game, who was I to argue? We squeezed between the bumpers of the cars in the driveway and went through the side gate like we knew exactly what we were doing.

And Marissa was right. There were a lot of people in the backyard. Trouble is, they were all old. Not old-old—I'm talking cocky-old. Hostile-old. You know, high school–old.

And all of a sudden we *didn't* look like we knew exactly what we were doing. We just stood there at the edge of the backyard, huddled up, wondering how cannibalistic this savage tribe was.

Music was blasting from a boom box on the patio, but no one was dancing. A lot of them were smoking cigarettes, and almost all of them were drinking. Beer. And pretty much, they weren't *doing* anything but talking and laughing, and smoking and drinking.

Straight ahead there was a building in the far corner of the yard—sort of a cross between a toolshed and a cabaña—and people seemed to go into it, but then not come out. And around the corner of the house, past the patio area, we could see through a sliding glass door into a room where people were shooting pool.

Skateboard or not, this felt wrong. The whole thing. And to tell you the truth, I was scared. For some reason, standing there on the edge of the lawn felt like standing on the edge of the world, and I sure didn't want to take the next step.

I whispered, "Let's get *out* of here."

Dot blinks a bunch and says, "No kidding."

And we're about to do a U-turn when Taylor comes out of the cabaña and spots us. We hurry back to the gate, but he chases after us, saying, "Hey! Wait up. Marissa, where you going?" And as soon as he catches up to us, he blocks our path and says, "Why don't you come in?"

Marissa says, "We...we just came for Sammy's skateboard. We can't stay."

Taylor puts his arm around her waist and says, "Aw, c'mon. Why don't you come in, just for a little bit? It's a party!"

Marissa shakes her head and says, "No...we've got to get back," but he guides her along, and before you know it we're at the front door again, only this time we walk right through.

Holly tugs on my arm and tries to tell me something, only I don't understand it. Then she wiggles her nose and points to Taylor. I mouth, What? and there she goes again, wiggling and pointing.

Finally, I pull her aside and ask, "What are you saying?"

"He's been smoking."

I look at her like, So?

"Grass."

I just stand there, staring at her. Then I whisper, "Marijuana?"

She nods.

"How do you know?"

"Believe me, nothing else smells like that."

Well, I did believe her. Not because I thought she'd ever smoked it, but because before she moved to our town she'd been in some pretty bad foster homes, and her life hasn't exactly been sheltered.

If I had been alone, I would've turned around and left right then. But Marissa was being swished down the drain by Taylor, and there was no way I was going to let that happen. So we followed them through the foyer, past a formal living room, down the hall, and back to the kitchen. And the funny thing is, there wasn't any smoke in the house at all. It was more like Potpourri Palace. Little dishes of it were everywhere, and the house smelled like roses and apples.

When we got to the kitchen, there were people sitting at the breakfast bar and just kind of hanging around the kitchen eating chips and drinking sodas. And they all seemed friendly and normal, just having a good time talking to each other. Taylor asks Marissa, "Would you like something to drink?"

She shakes her head.

He pops a potato chip in his mouth and says, "This down here's the rec room. You play pool?"

Marissa shakes her head, then looks over her shoulder at me and says, "But Sammy does."

I look at her like, Why did you say *that*? because I play pool about as well as I embroider. Marissa pulls a face back at me, which means HELP! so what can I do? The ball's already in motion—we're going in.

The rec room wasn't the Edge of the World. It was more like the *shore* of the Edge of the World. People were playing pool and darts, and along one wall there were old video games like Pac-Man and Space Invaders. There were a few beer cans, but Holly's nose wasn't twitching, and we weren't choking on smoke.

Taylor's still got his arm around Marissa, and when we step down into the rec room, who's sitting on a saggy leather couch with a beer in her hand?

Heather.

And I don't know what cooked her carrots more, the sight of me at the party or Taylor's arm around Marissa. She ducks the beer behind the couch like we're her parents, then snaps out of her seat and struts over to us.

Taylor tries to be casual about it, but the fact is that one minute his arm's around Marissa, and the next minute it's not. He says to Heather, "Where's Tenille?"

She looks at him like she's a rotisserie and he's one bald and basted bird. "She had to pee."

He says, "Be cool, Heather. Be cool," but she's not about to turn the heat down. She pulls him aside and says, "I can't believe you let them in!" and then sizzles and spatters until finally he puts his hands up and says, "Look, they're here now, so just deal." Then he sees a guy come in through the sliding glass door with a cigarette in his hand. And even though the guy's got whiskers where Taylor's still got fuzz, Taylor calls, "Hey! Outta here with that! No smoking in the house."

The guy calls, "Hey, dude, where's Karl?"

"He went to get supplies."

"Dude! I hope he doesn't take as long as he did last time—he was gone for like an *hour*, dude. We're dry out here!"

"He'll be back...Now get out of here with that, man!"

The minute he's gone, Heather's little sidekick Tenille comes stumbling down the steps. She's wearing a dark blue stretch skirt that's shrunk *way* up her legs and heavy black shoes with platform soles. She takes one look at us, then turns to Heather and cracks up. And as she clomps her way over to Heather, she says, "Tell me I'm dreamin'," only it sounds more like one long, seasick word. Then she starts laughing.

Now this is not a pretty sight. I mean, Tenille doesn't exactly come off as a multi-linguist when she's sober, but this was like taking a muzzle off a mule. And hearing her hee-hawing was *embarrassing*.

Tenille, though, thought she was being smooth and suave. She stands by Heather and says to Taylor, "I guess every picnic has its ants...the question is, how to get rid of them?"

Heather says through her teeth, "He *invited* them."

Tenille says, "Oh-ho-*ho!*" and then brays some more.

Finally, I say, "Look. Could I just get my skateboard? Then we'll make everyone happy and get out of here."

Taylor looks at me. "What's the rush?" Then he turns

to Marissa and says, "Can I get you something to eat? Something to drink?"

Of course the person Heather's really mad at is Taylor. But does she take it out on him? Or even Marissa? No. She turns to him and says, "I really don't think this is the kind of party you want to invite *fourth* graders to," and then glares at me.

Taylor says, "Heather…" but she's only warming up. She points to me and says, "You know what a narc that girl is, you know she's sneaky and nerdy and just…just… *weird*. Why stop with her? Why not invite the geeks off the street? Why not just open your door and say, 'Hey! You ugly and annoying? Come on in, destroy my party!'"

Then all of a sudden from behind me this voice says, "Cool it, Heather! Either get back in your cage or get out of here!"

I knew I'd heard the voice before, but when I whipped around and saw Taylor's friend with the baggy pants, I couldn't quite believe it. He gives me a smile that's really half a scowl and says, "Not that I don't think you can hold your own."

Heather does back down. Fast. And Taylor's looking pretty relieved, let me tell you. He rubs his hands together and says, "Well. Why don't you guys shoot some pool or play darts or something? I'll get some munchies."

Taylor zips off to the kitchen, leaving the rest of us standing there like tortilla chips in bean dip, none of us wanting to be the first one scooped.

Finally, Marissa says, "I think I'll go play Pac-Man," and Dot and Holly say, "Me, too," and look at me like, Well?

But I don't want to play Pac-Man. I don't want to play pool or darts. I want to get my skateboard and get *out* of there. So I say, "You go ahead. I'll be right there." They hesitate for a minute, but I shoo them off, and when the three of them are gone, I turn my back on Heather and say to Baggy, "Could you please get Taylor to give me my skateboard? That's the only reason we're here."

He looks at me like I'm speaking French. "Your skateboard? You still on about that?"

"Look, he called and told us to come to the party so he could give us the skateboard. Do you know where it is?"

Now he doesn't say, *Oui, oui!* but we do seem to be talking the same language. "I can't believe Jake's giving it back after all of that."

"Jake's Snake, right?"

He hesitates, then kind of grins and nods.

"All I know is Taylor told Marissa that they'd scraped off the paint and realized it was mine after all. Is Snake, uh, *Jake* even here?"

"Oh, he's around here somewhere." Baggy Boy looks over one shoulder, then the other, and he's about to say something else when Heather butts in. "Aren't you going to turn into a pumpkin or something if you're not home by midnight?" She looks at her watch and sneers, "Better hurry."

I snap, "Well, who put a Stupidity Spell on *you*? Can't you see I'm *trying* to get out of here? You think I *want* to be in the same room as you and the Witless Wonder?" I eye Tenille and mutter, "Like she had any brain cells left to kill off."

Heather turns to Baggy and says, "She's gonna narc," but he's not looking too worried. He's standing there cracking up. She gives him a one-hand shove to the chest and says, "Do you hear me? She's gonna narc!"

He's still laughing. "A Stupidity Spell…the Witless Wonder…!"

She shoves him again, this time with both hands. "Stop it! I'm serious!"

He just ignores her and says to me, "C'mon. Let's go find Jake." And as soon as we round the corner out of the rec room, he does something no guy has ever done to me before.

He turns around and smiles at me, then reaches out and takes my hand.

TWELVE

I tried to yank my hand back. I mean, I didn't even *know* the guy, and here he was, holding my hand. But he smiled at me and just held it tighter. "C'mon, Sammy. Relax!"

"*Relax?* Excuse me, but I feel like I'm in the middle of some adolescent ambush. Heather's here, there's beer everywhere, there're boys as big as grizzlies out there smokin' dope, and you're telling me to *relax?*"

And what's he do? He stops, looks at me, and laughs. "Adolescent ambush? Are you always this funny?"

I just stare at him. I mean, there he is, holding my hand, telling me I'm funny when, in fact, I'm never funny around boys. Ever. What I am is tongue-tied. But apparently my tongue has taken this opportunity to un-ravel, because it can't seem to stop flapping. I say, "I'm not funny, I'm serious! And how'd you know my name, anyway?"

He pulls me out of the way of a girl heading down the hallway. "How'd I know your *name?*"

"Yeah. I never told you what it was, and I don't think anyone even said it. This morning or now."

"Well, I've *known* your name. You're...uh...kinda notorious."

"Notorious? How am I notorious? What's that sup-posed to mean?"

He grins and says, "At school."

"You go to William Rose?"

"Never noticed me, huh?"

I shake my head.

"Well, I've noticed you."

I can feel myself turn red. I mean, I'm not sure if he's making fun of me or not. Then he adds, "And Heather talks about you."

Oh yeah. Heather. "Well, if you're so tight with Heather, why are you holding my hand?"

That startled him. And it kind of startled me, too. And for a second there I thought he was going to let go, but he decides to hang on. "First of all, Heather and I are *not* tight. Second off...I don't know"—he shrugs and grins—"I like you."

I pull my hand away. "I don't even know your name!"

He laughs and says, "Hey! Well, I guess you don't. But I can fix that." He crosses his arms, looks up at the ceil-ing, and says, "My name's Casey, I live at 782 Golden Oak Circle, I'm in the eighth grade at William Rose Junior High, I like skateboarding, mountain biking, skiing, and baseball. My favorite color's green, and if my dad would let me, I'd eat macaroni and salsa for dinner every night."

"Macaroni and *salsa*?"

"It's god-like."

I laugh and say, "I'll have to try that sometime. Macaroni and *cheese* and salsa? Or just macaroni and salsa?"

"Gotta have the cheese." He grins at me and says, "But

we were on a quest for your skateboard, weren't we?"

I nod. "So where's Jake-the-Snake?"

He laughs. "Don't let *him* hear you say that. Jake's fine, Snake's fine, but Jake-the-Snake is like The End. And I don't know—he's got to be around here somewhere."

So off we went, hands safely in pockets, cruising the halls for Jake-the-you-know-what. But after checking every room in the house and looking in the backyard, Casey says, "Well, you *know*…it might still be in Ben's truck. I saw it there earlier."

So we go out to the driveway and there, looking like a big steel elephant squeezed up alongside the fence, is the same primer-gray paddy wagon that had rounded up Taylor and his gang that morning. The hood's warm and the truck's making little tinging and pinging sounds, settling in, and while I check out the bed of the truck, Casey tries the doors.

The cab's locked up tight, and there's nothing in the bed except a nearly bald spare tire, a couple of quarts of oil, and some leaves and twigs. Then Casey looks inside and calls, "There it is! On the floor."

"Really?"

"Yeah. I thought it might be. I saw him put it up there this morning after Ben brought us back from town."

"You mean it's been there all day?"

"I don't know. I guess so."

"Has *Jake* been here all day?"

Casey shrugs and says, "You got me. I had to take off. But Taylor kinda wanted Jake to stick around so his mom wouldn't blow too bad. Anyway, I think Ben had to work today, so if it's in there now, it probably has been all day."

"And if it's been in the truck all day…"

He looks at me and he knows exactly what I'm thinking. He mutters, "…then nobody's scraped off the paint."

"Exactly. And nobody's planning to give me back my skateboard."

He says, "We don't know this. Maybe they did and…they put it back in here. Maybe…" and while he's reaching for an answer, I'm looking at him like, Right. So likely.

He knows it's sounding kind of weak, so he throws his hands up and says, "I don't know! Why would he tell you that if it wasn't true?"

"The reason's name is Marissa."

"Marissa?" The answer clicked like the right key in a padlock, but you could tell he didn't *want* it to fit. "Naw…" Then he gets a bright idea. "Hey! Ben stashes a key somewhere around…" He dives down and looks at the underside of the truck, but he never does say "here."

So I figure I'll get down and help him look. I squat, then crane my neck around, not exactly knowing where you'd go about stashing a key under a car.

Casey says, "It's gotta be here…unless Karl didn't put it back."

"Karl? Does he drive?"

"Just got his license. Ben about has a meltdown every time Karl takes the truck, but Ben's like that."

Casey lies down on his back and scoots under the car just

in front of the wheel, so I ask, "Wouldn't the key just fall off if you put it under there?" He doesn't answer, so I lie on my back and scoot under the car, too. "Wouldn't it?"

He looks at me and laughs. Not mean or anything. Just happy laughing. I kind of laugh back and say, "What? I'm sorry. I just don't get it. Where would you hide a key in this mess?"

He's still smiling. "In a key keeper. A little tin case about the size of a matchbox with a magnet on one side."

Now I get it. So I start looking around for a little tin case about the size of a matchbox that's sucking up to something metal, only when I happen to look over at Casey, he's not looking at the car. He's looking at me. He laughs and says, "What *are* you doing down here?"

I look at him like he's got spaghetti for brains. "I'm looking for the key...?"

"You must really want that skateboard."

Well, I do, but to tell you the truth, I wasn't really thinking about the board at the moment—I was just hunting for a key. And I'm about to tell him so when something goes *splat!* right on my cheek.

Now if you've ever wrestled yourself under a vehicle in the middle of the night to find a key that doesn't belong to you, you know that the first thing you're going to do when some strange fluid drips on your face is jerk your head up and bang it. Hard.

Casey says, "Oh man, are you all right?"

I scoot out from under the truck holding my forehead. "I'm fine."

"Are you *sure*?"

I sit there on the ground and say, "Yeah. But I think they could build a ski resort around this bump on my head."

He tries not to laugh, but he can't help it. "You're a mess!"

I get up and look in one of the elephant-ear mirrors, and sure enough, I'm a mess. Not only is Mount Everest erupting on my forehead, but it's smudged black with oil and grime. And then there's the splat, which has nicely run all the way down my cheek to my jawbone, leaving a faint pink trail. I wipe off some of the splat with my fingertips and rub my thumb against it, trying to figure out how a truck like that could possibly contain anything *pink*, when Casey asks, "Is that tranny fluid?"

I wipe off some more and say, "I don't know."

So he comes right up, swipes my cheek with a finger, rubs it against his thumb, then holds it up to his nose and *smells* it. "Yup. Tranny fluid."

I take a whiff, too, and it does smell different. Kind of sweet. "Is that from the transmission?"

"Yeah. Ben's truck leaks all *kinds*."

He stretches the sleeve of his flannel shirt over his palm and cleans my cheek with it, but I still feel greasy and grimy. "Thanks, but I think I ought to wash this stuff off. Is there a bathroom I can use?"

"C'mon, I'll show you."

As I'm following him back to the house, I notice that his flannel's got dust and little pebbles stuck to it, so I say, "Hold still," and swat off his back. He does the same for me, only I guess I'm a bigger mess than he was because he starts swatting off my sleeves, too, and before I can stop him, he whacks my sore arm.

I jump away with a yelp, and he says, "What? What? Did I *hurt* you?"

I pull up my sweatshirt sleeve and show him my bandaged arm. "From this morning…?"

"Oh yeah…! Sorry." He grins and says, "You've had a real couch-potato day, haven't you?" then leads me into the house.

I lock myself up in the bathroom, get the water really hot, then scrub my face down. And as I'm drying off, I realize that the voices I'm hearing through the wall aren't party voices—they're angry voices.

I scoot up close to the wall behind the toilet, but I can't make out any words. Just muffled, angry sounds. So I put my ear smack-dab against the wallpaper. And now I *can* make out bits and pieces, but nothing that makes any sense. And after a minute of this, I tell myself I'm being stupid. I mean, why do I care what they're fighting about? If it's not about my skateboard, then it's none of my business, right? So I arrange my bangs over Mount Everest, then switch off the light and head out.

And who's waiting for me in the hallway?

Nobody.

Then I notice the heel of a boot sticking out from around the corner at the end of the hall. And I stand there a minute trying to decide whether I should go down the hall to see if it's Casey or back to the party to find Marissa.

I wind up inching down the hall, and when I get close

enough, I see that it's Casey, all right, and he's positioned like a sprinter, leaning way around the corner with his ear against a door.

He sees me and snaps upright, *boing!* then tries to act casual. "Looks like you got it all off."

I nod and ask, "What are they arguing about? I could hear them clear through the bathroom wall."

Casey shakes his head. "You got me, but you're right— they're raging in there."

"Who is it? Taylor and his brother?"

"No, it's Karl and Ben. I got that much." He snorts and says, "And I don't think now would be a very good time to ask either one of them for the key!"

The door flies open, then slams shut. And even though no one came out, it felt like the hall had been blasted by a blowtorch of angry words. Casey whispers, "Let's jam," and we hightail it out of there.

When we get to the rec room, Casey spots Taylor playing Pac-Man with Marissa and says, "Hang back for a minute. I'm going to straighten this with Taylor. This whole thing is getting really stupid."

Holly and Dot are off in a corner, looking at a gallery of team pictures hanging on the wall, so while Casey goes to talk to Taylor, I zip over to Holly and Dot. Right away they attack me with, "Where have you *been*? We were starting to think you'd left!"

I toss a look in Casey's direction and say, "We've been trying to get my skateboard back." Casey pulls Taylor aside, so I wave Marissa over and say, "But I don't think it's going to happen."

Dot asks, "Why not?"

Now I'd have answered her right away, only as I turn to tell her, I notice someone in a picture on the wall, right over her shoulder. He's standing by a swimming pool with a great big grin on his face, holding up one end of a trophy while Karl Briggs holds up the other. And I know it's him, because I'd recognize him anywhere—bundled in ski clothes or streaking in Speedos—it's Marissa's cousin Brandon.

And what's weird about seeing him in the picture is that it feels like he's watching me. Like he's grinning at *me*. I move a little to the left and back to the right, but no matter which way I shift, there he is, grinning away, right at me.

Dot says, "What are you doing?"

"Huh...? Oh, nothing."

"So why isn't it going to happen?"

"Why isn't...what?"

"Sammy! You were telling us you weren't going to get the skateboard back. Why not?"

I turn away from the picture and say, "Because it was just Marissa bait. My skateboard's in Taylor's brother's truck. Apparently it's been there all day."

"So?"

"So nobody's scraped the paint off, nobody's seen my initials, and nobody's planning to return it. Taylor just said that to get Marissa to come to the party."

Marissa stares at me and I stare at her, and finally she says, "Well, if that's true, let's get out of here!"

Taylor and Casey seem to be having a pretty serious

discussion over by the Pac-Man game, but it's easy to see that Taylor's the one calling the shots. And I'm thinking, Yeah, let's just forget it and go, when I notice Heather whispering with Tenille, kind of blocking the door to the kitchen.

Going through them would be like trying to walk through barbed wire, and really, I wasn't up for that. I'd been beat up enough for one day already. Then it hits me that there *is* another way out. I just have to step over the Edge of the World to get there.

Dot sees me looking toward the backyard and says, "Oh, Sammy, no. Let's not go that way."

I nod at Heather and say, "You'd rather go out *that* way?"

Holly says, "There are four of us and two of them. And Tenille doesn't even really count, so let's just plow 'em over."

They're right, of course. Four against one and a half weren't bad odds—what was Heather going to do? Throw earrings at us? Still, I had scars to prove that tangling with her could leave you seriously gouged, and I wanted to get out of there in one piece.

But suddenly it's too late anyway. Casey and Taylor are right beside us, and Taylor starts laying it on, thick and sweet. "Sorry about the misunderstanding. I guess Jake's kind of flakin' out. I don't know what the deal is with the skateboard. Maybe we'll get it from him tomorrow."

Marissa just looks down, so Taylor says, "That doesn't mean you have to leave. Why don't you stay and ring in the New Year?"

At first, Marissa doesn't say anything. She just stands there with her arms crossed and her eyes to the ground. Then, very quietly, she says, "Why'd you lie to me?"

He wasn't expecting that. No one was expecting that. And while we're all looking at Marissa with our eyebrows up and our jaws down, Taylor takes his first swing. He stutters, "Lie to...why do you think I...I didn't lie to you!"

Strike one. She looks straight at him and pitches another. "Then get the skateboard."

He swings again. "Okay, but I...I've got to clear it with Snake first."

Strike two.

She keeps right on looking at him. "Why? I thought this was his idea."

"Well, it was *our* idea, but—"

"But he doesn't know anything about it, right?"

"No...I mean...sure he does. But I can't just give it to you without telling him first, right? I mean, it's his board."

Strike three, and we are out of there. Marissa says, "No, it's *Sammy's* board." She pushes past him saying, "Silly me to think you were trying to do the right thing."

He says, "I...Look, I...," but it's too late. There's no way he's going to make it to first base with Marissa.

The rest of us stand there for a few seconds, stunned, while Marissa marches away. We snap out of it and chase after her, and I want to slap a high-five on her for what she's done, but by the time I catch up to her, we've got the Guerrilla Girls to deal with.

Marissa says, "Heather, please. Get out of the way."

Tenille's trying to act all tough and together, but really she looks seasick swaying there in her platform shoes. Heather smirks at Marissa like, Make me, but she doesn't say a word, she just stands there.

I take a step forward and say, "Look, I thought you wanted us to leave. Why don't you—"

Out of nowhere, Casey grabs my hand and pulls me up the steps behind him, saying, "Jesus, Heather—get out of the way!" And when we're past the doorway, he keeps right on holding my hand, then turns around and says to Heather, "Would you work on not being such an embarrassment?"

Now I've seen Heather mad before. Lots of times. I've also seen her upset and shocked. But I've never seen her mad, upset, *and* shocked, all at the same time.

She was, though, all three. And for once her eyes weren't shooting darts at me. She was looking from Casey's hand to his face, and for the first time since I've known her, Heather Acosta was dumbfounded.

Casey guides me through the kitchen and down the hall, saying, "This whole situation's jacked. I can't even believe it." He turns to me. "It might not happen tonight, but I'll get you your skateboard. I promise."

All of a sudden we can hear gears grinding and tires squealing out of the driveway, and then Karl comes slamming into the house through the front door. He practically plows us over going down the hall, and as we watch him go, Casey says, "Not a good time to be asking to get in the truck."

I laugh. "No kidding."

He walks us outside and says, "Not that we could anyway. That must've been Ben peeling out of here." He looks at me. "But if I do manage to get your board, how can I get ahold of you?"

Now my tongue's acting normal. I can't think of a thing to say. I mean, what am I supposed to do, give him Grams' number? That would fly like a zeppelin with her. So I'm standing there like an idiot, not knowing what to say, when Dot comes to my rescue. "You could bring it over to my house. Sammy's spending the weekend. It's right up the road, on Meadow Lane. Just follow the signs to DeVries Nursery."

"DeVries Nursery?"

"That's right."

He nods and looks real serious when he says, "Okay, I will," then gives me a little wave and says, "See ya."

The minute he goes back inside, all three of them grab me and say, "What is going on!?"

"What do you mean?"

"Sammy...he was holding your hand!"

I blush. Completely. Dot says, "Well...? Do you like him?"

"I don't know! I don't even know him!"

Marissa says, "Then why did you let him hold your hand?"

I look straight at her. "This from the girl who let *Taylor* put his arm around her?"

Now it's her turn to blush. "Sorry."

I kind of scowl and say, "Me, too." Then I get on my

bike and sigh. "It's all just…confusing. Casey's…I don't know. *Nice*."

I said it to regret it. Dot practically squeals, "She *does* like him!" and since she's riding right beside me, I give her a little punch in the arm. But all that does is make her wobble and say, "You *do!* I can tell!"

They teased me the whole way home. And I kept telling them to shut up, but it was no use; it only made them tease me more. And by the time we turned down Meadow Lane, I was really sorry I'd ever gone to Taylor's. I mean, my skateboard meant a lot to me, but life was confusing enough without getting tangled up with, you know…

Boys.

THIRTEEN

Lights were still on when we rode up to Dot's house. We parked our bikes around by the carriage house and I asked, "Are we in trouble for getting back so late?"

Dot said, "We shouldn't be…," and I'm just thinking, Wow, that's amazing! because I'd be in a whole lot more than trouble if it were Grams waiting up, when Dot adds, "I called them from Lucinda's house."

"You *did*?"

She looks at me like I'm squirrel bait. "Of course."

"When?"

"While you were getting the diary…?" She shakes her head and says, "They'd have been worried sick if I hadn't. I promised them we'd be home before midnight, so we're okay."

To tell you the truth, I'd forgotten all about Moustache Mary's diary. But I had the copy right there in Hudson's saddlebag, and with everything that had happened at Taylor's, well, the thought of reading about a gunslinging woman in a moustache seemed like just what I needed. I said, "Wait for me, okay?" then raced inside the carriage house to stash the diary with my stuff.

After that, we tiptoed into the house, but Dot's parents were wide awake, sitting next to each other on the couch.

Anneke's head was in one lap and Beppie's head was in the other, and both girls were sound asleep. Mrs. DeVries whispers, "Glad you girls are back."

Dot says, "Sorry it took so long."

"That's all right—New Year's only comes once a year." She scoots forward to the edge of the couch and cradles Anneke in her arms. "Thanks so much for having Stan and Troy call. You'll have to tell us more about the fire in the morning."

Dot looks at the clock and asks, "Aren't you staying up?"

Mr. DeVries shakes his head. "We watched the ball drop on TV."

"But that's in a different time zone…!"

He picks up Beppie. "It's all relative, *ja?*" He smiles and says, "Pleasant dreams."

Dot's mom gives her a kiss on the forehead. "Your father put a flashlight out there for each of you, but you're still welcome to sleep inside if you'd like. It's getting pretty cold, so maybe long johns are in order?"

The minute they're gone, Dot whispers, "Anyone else want some *oliebollen?* I'm starved!"

Well, I was, too. We all were. So we sat around the table eating powdered-sugar grenades, talking first about Pioneer Village and Taylor's party, and then about Mary's cabin and what we were going to do the next day about the missing gas can. And when every last crumb was gone and we were all talked out, Dot looks up at the cuckoo clock on the wall and says, "It's almost midnight, should I let him out?"

Holly asks, "Let who out?"

"Cuckoo."

Now this is no shoebox cuckoo clock. It's as massive as a moose with antlers to match. And it seemed that a clock like that would bark or growl or *roar*, so I said, "Sure!"

Dot jumps up and pries down a little metal lever, then stands back. "Hope it doesn't wake up Mom and Dad!"

We stood there, watching the big hand tick toward the little hand, and when they were both pointing straight up, out pops the bird crying, "Cuckoo!" twelve times.

It *was* loud—really loud. Not quite a roar, but close. And when the bird went back in for the last time, Dot pried up the lever quick as can be and we all busted up.

Now you may think it's not much of a celebration, eating fried grenades and watching a wooden bird roar, but it was the best New Year's I'd ever had. I was with my friends, and we were happy just to be together talking and cuckooing in the New Year. And when I thought about Heather and Tenille and all the people at the Briggses' house, imagining what they were doing right then, I was really glad I wasn't there.

We hung around a little longer, then Dot passed out long johns and we brushed our teeth and went to bed. And I know I *should've* been tired, but I wasn't. I was wired. And long after Dot and Holly and Marissa had fallen asleep, I was still lying there in the dark, thinking about everything that had happened. About the fire and the gas can, and what I was going to say to Officer Borsch in the morning. About Lucinda and Penny, and Kevin and Dallas. About the Murdocks with their zitty butler and their steamy tempers. And Casey. My brain wouldn't stop coming back to Casey. And every time it did, my stupid cheek would tingle. Right where he'd touched it.

Now, I'd much rather think about police and pigs and pioneer people than some guy, so when my brain just wouldn't behave itself, I decided to give it something else to do.

I dug Moustache Mary's journal out of my stuff, scrunched inside the sleeping bag so my head was covered, and clicked on the flashlight.

At first, it was way too bright, but after rustling around for a bit I got comfortable, and before you know it, I was on the high plains with Mary heading west.

And really, it was the most amazing thing I'd ever read. Some of the entries were really short. Like:

> *April the 14th—Traveled 20 miles and camped. Roads bad. Feed scarce.*
> *April 15th—Rainy and cold. The country so far has been broken and wet, with a clay subsoil.*
> *April 17th—In camp waiting for the roads to dry and settle.*

But in others she wrote about the people she was traveling with—the emigrants—and her hopes and fears for the "fertile and earthly paradise" she'd heard missionaries and mountaineers talk about. And it didn't take long for the name Murdock to appear.

Lucinda had told the story just the way Mary had written it, except reading the story in Mary's own hand sent shivers **through** me. It's like I could hear her voice; could practically **see** Lewis Murdock rip the moustache off her lip and **hear him** cry, "Impostor!"; could feel her tiredness after **walking** twenty miles beside the wagon train, and her worry that Ezekiel was "worn to the bone."

There were words and phrases that, at first, I didn't understand, or didn't recognize right away because of the spelling but, after a few pages, started making sense. Like:

> *We bilt a fire of good dry chips and cookd a fine supper of grouse, soup, and soda bread.*

I knew grouse was a bird, but I didn't realize that chips were dried buffalo poop until I was pages and pages into the journal, and then I still couldn't quite believe it. I mean, burning poop to heat your soup doesn't sound too appetizing to me.

And Mary talked about people dying like it was something that happened every day. In one entry she says,

> *Poor Jim Applegate's famly buried him in the rut, in hopes that Injuns wouldn't see to dig him up.*

So I kept trying to figure out what a "rut" was. And then a few pages later I realized that it was the path left by wagon wheels. I had to stop and think about that a minute. I mean, what a choice—being dug up and scalped or having your grave run over again and again by wagon wheels.

Mary did mention the gold. Several times. Sometimes

she called it "the coins," sometimes "the gold," and once she called it "our family treasure." And she thought that the Murdocks "were envious over it" because they had seen "the weight of the satchel" when she'd used a piece to trade for supplies at a post in Fort Hall. After that she kept it "secreted from those scoundrels" and felt it best that even Ezekiel didn't know where she'd stashed it.

So there *was* gold. And sometime after I read about supplies being scarce and Mary being "sorry for having to shoot" Lewis Murdock for dipping into her barrel of flour, I started wondering if it was the flour he was after, or if maybe, just maybe, he was searching for her gold.

I read the whole journal, cover to cover. And on the last page was the riddle Dallas had mentioned. It was all by itself, and in handwriting that was still Mary's, but not as smooth and flowing. Like it had been added later, when she was much older. I kept re-reading it, trying to make sense of it:

> Where the ridge meets the rock and the rock meets the ground
> The box is shallow, black and crowned
> Not far in, left and high
> Gold and silver, warm inside

* * *

The next thing I know, Dot's flipping back my sleeping bag saying, "Sammy…Hey, Sammy…Are you going to sleep all day? Breakfast is on the table."

"Wh…what?"

She sees my flashlight and says, "Have you had that thing on all night?" Then she sees the diary. "You were *reading* in there?"

The last thing I felt like doing was getting up. But after I grunted and pulled the bag back over my head, Dot says, "You were going to call Officer Borsch, remember? First thing in the morning?"

That was true. And part of me was mad at Dot for saying it because she *knew* it would get me out of bed. I flipped the cover off and moaned, "You're a brat."

She laughs, "I just don't want you to miss out. Mom made *appelflappen*."

"*Appelflappen*? Let me guess…that's some kind of flying Dutch apple?"

"Ha, ha. C'mon, they're great. They're like apple pancakes, only round like a ball, and you eat them with jam. You can have them with syrup if you want, we've got syrup…or just powdered sugar…or jam, syrup, *and* sugar…or even—"

"I'm coming, all right? I'm coming." I raked my hair back and flipped it through a rubberband, then reached for my clothes.

"Oh, don't worry about that—you look fine."

Now the long johns Dot had lent me weren't ones I'd have picked out for myself. I didn't mind so much that they were old and tattered and missing buttons. And underwear-white is pretty standard when it comes to long johns, so it wasn't *that*. It was the swooshing red hearts that went from head to toe that looked ridiculous. On me, anyway.

And during the night I had been glad to wear swooshy-hearted underwear. They'd kept me nice and toasty. But they weren't exactly the kind of thing I'd want to *socialize* in.

I said, "It'll only take a minute..."

She grabs me by the arm and yanks. "Good grief, Sammy. My brothers are over at Marko's, my parents are in their robes...everyone's waiting!"

So I shuffle into the house with my high-tops dangling laces, double-checking to make sure all those swooshy hearts are fastened in places where they might be trying to further embarrass me.

When we get to the dining room, sure enough, everyone's waiting with a fork in one hand and a knife in the other, looking like they're going to start pounding the table for food. Especially Anneke and Beppie.

Mr. DeVries sees me and says, "At last!" and the minute Dot and I slide into our chairs he proclaims, *"Smakelijk eten,"* and everyone digs in.

Marissa says through a mouthful, "How come you were so zonked?"

Dot answers for me. "She was up all night reading that diary."

Holly asks, "Really? Was it any good?"

All of a sudden I didn't feel tired anymore. "It's the most amazing thing I've ever read. It's almost spooky."

"What do you mean, spooky?" Marissa asks. "'Cause of the ghost?"

"No. Because it feels so real. It's like going back in a time machine or something. I mean, Lucinda told us how

Mary passed herself off as a man, and about the trouble she had with the Murdocks, but she didn't talk about the *trip*. It was treacherous! And the farther they got from Missouri, the worse it got. They didn't ride in the wagons, they walked *next* to them."

Dot asks, "Why?"

"They didn't want to wear out their pack animals. In one stretch they went days without water, and when they finally came to some, it tasted so bad that they couldn't get the livestock to drink it. And since the animals were dehydrated, they made coffee out of it to disguise the flavor so the animals would drink it."

Dot's mom wrinkles up her forehead. "They wouldn't drink the water, but they'd drink *coffee?* That must've been some pretty foul water."

"And then a couple of days later they got trapped in a rainstorm where it thundered and lightninged and sleeted so hard that they were blinded and soaked and blown over by the wind. So they went from dehydration to having so much water that they had to float their wagons across a river."

"Those things *floated?*" Holly shakes her head. "You'd think they'd go down like a rock."

"Yeah, you'd think. But Mary wrote how they tacked buffalo hide to the bottom of the wagon, took off the wheels, got everything inside up as high as they could, and then floated it across. Some of the cattle got spooked and a couple of the emigrants lost everything, but Mary's wagon was fine."

Dot's dad says, "Buffalo hide. Now isn't that resourceful?"

Then he asks, "Did she write anything about Indians in that journal?"

"Lots. They got attacked a few times, and once the Indians lit a brushfire to spook their livestock so they'd run off and be captured. But she also writes about Indians who traded with them, and others that were helpful. It was the Murdocks she was afraid of. Much more so than the Indians."

Mrs. DeVries shakes her head and says, "It seems that if you'd gone through hardships like that you'd find a common bond. I can't imagine living that way. These people walked two thousand miles to reach their destination. Two thousand miles!"

"Mary says something in the journal like 'the only reason they can feign honesty is because there's nothing to steal, and the only reason they're industrious is because their choice is work or starve.' At first, she calls them 'Mr. Murdock' and 'the brother Murdock,' but about a third of the way through she starts calling them 'the evil Murdock clan,' and says something like 'They were just after the mother lode and were wanting to get rich by hook or by crook.'"

Dot's dad says, "People can have different motivations for making the same journey, *ja?*"

Mrs. DeVries says, "Still, I think it's a shame."

I'd been talking so much that I hadn't really eaten anything. So while they're discussing the Huntleys and the Murdocks, I stuff away like a squirrel before winter. And right when I'm good and double-cheeked, there's a sharp *knock-knock-knock* on the door.

Now maybe living illegally at Grams' has made me jumpy when it comes to people knocking unexpectedly, because I sure jumped. And when I jumped, I choked. And then I started coughing. And coughing and coughing and coughing.

Mrs. DeVries says, "My goodness!" and Dot adds, "Are you all right?"

My face is red and my eyes are watery, but I'm so grateful not to have sprayed the place with apple mush that I nod and say, "I'm fine." Then I whisper, "Who do you think's at the door?"

A light bulb comes on, *boing!* over Marissa's head. "You're worried that it's Casey!"

I want to say, "No, I'm not!" but the words won't seem to come out. Instead, I turn a darker shade of red. I point to the gaps and *holes* in my long johns and say, "Look at me, okay? I'd be worried if it were the *dog* catcher!"

We all laugh about that, but the minute Mr. DeVries comes back into the room and looks at me, I about choke again because there's no doubt about it.

Someone's there to see *me.*

FOURTEEN

I look to Dot for help. "I can't go to the door like this!"

Mr. DeVries says, "I wouldn't keep him waiting if I were you." He looks at his wife. "It's a police officer."

"A *police* officer?"

I whisper, "Did you guys already call about the gas can?"

They all shake their heads.

Mrs. DeVries asks, "What gas can? What is going on, Margaret?"

Dot stands up and follows me to the door, saying, "Nothing bad, Mom. Don't worry."

Mr. DeVries lowers his voice. "Well, he appears to be in ill humor—I wouldn't keep him waiting."

It was Officer Borsch, all right. And I could've been dressed in a fancy formal for all the attention he paid my long johns. No Hello, no I'm sorry to intrude, Sammy. He just jumps right in with, "You *promised* me."

I shake my head and ask, "What did I do?"

He cocks his thumb toward the porch, motioning me to step outside. So I follow him out the door and down the steps, until we're in a small clearing of dried grass and oak leaves. He stops and looks around a little, then puts his hands on his hips. Right above his gunbelt.

Marissa, Dot, and Holly are hanging back on the porch,

kind of behind me, Officer Borsch's squad car is parked off the side of the road beneath an oak tree behind *him*, and I'm standing in a patch of dead grass in swooshy hearts and floppy high-tops facing the Borsch-man like we're set for a duel.

I ask him, *"What?"*

"I'm debating doing you a favor."

"A *favor*? Okaaaaaaay. Could you maybe explain that a little?"

He looks at me, kind of snorts, then looks down, shakes his head, and snorts again. "I intercepted a complaint."

"A complaint? What kind of complaint?"

He takes a deep breath. "That someone was nosing around the fire site."

"Someone? And right away you figured that someone was *me*?"

Officer Borsch shakes his head and says, "Sorry, but it sounded like you to me. Are you saying it wasn't?"

"Well, we didn't *disturb* anything..."

"Hmmm!" He nods like, I knew it!

"Really! We didn't!" I scowled at him. "Who complained, anyway?"

He hesitates. Then he admits, "I don't have that information."

"Oh, but you believe them over me...!"

"Look, Sammy. Just stay off the Huntley property—is that clear?"

"But Officer Borsch!"

"I'm serious, Sammy. Aside from breaking your word to me, you have no business going over there."

I take a step forward and say, "I did *not* break my word to you. I stayed out of the way. I didn't bug the firemen, and I didn't go snooping around...well, not much anyway."

"Uh-huh."

"It's true! Look, Lucinda *wanted* us there, and we would've left right after she fell asleep, only then we found the gas can and..."

"What gas can?"

"The *empty* gas can that still smelled like gasoline. And for once I wasn't going to touch the evidence. I was going to get *you* instead, but when we went to the house to ask Kevin to use the phone, nobody came to the door. And when we finally went back to where the can had been, it was gone."

While I'm talking, his face is falling. And I can practically hear him thinking, Oh no-no-no, not again..., because he's getting the picture that a little click of the heels is not going to send me back to Kansas. He says, "Gone? As in somebody took it?"

I nod.

"Are you sure?"

"I'm sure."

He looks up to the porch, and Holly says, "It's true. Every word."

"How much time elapsed?"

"Between the time we found the can and the time we realized it was gone?"

"That's right."

"Twenty minutes?" I look to the others. "You think that's right?"

They shrug and nod, so I say, "More than fifteen and less than thirty."

"So why didn't you call me when you got home?"

I sigh and say, "It was late, and then we had some other minor emergencies over in Pioneer Village to take care of. I was going to call you right after we got done with breakfast."

One of his eyebrows arches up. "You weren't tangled up in that mess out on Wagonwheel Road, were you?"

"What mess?"

"Never mind."

Just then I hear someone behind me gasp, and when I turn around, both Dot and Marissa have their hands in front of their mouths, and Holly's got "Uh-oh!" written all over her face. I look to where they're staring—past Officer Borsch, past his squad car, out to the dirt road—and there, with my skateboard under his arm, is Casey.

I about died. And maybe it was stupid, but the first thing I tried to do was hide. And since we were in a clearing and the only thing to hide *behind* was Officer Borsch, that's what I tried to do. Trouble is, he kept *moving*. And when he finally managed to ditch me, Casey had walked over, and there we were, face to face.

He doesn't say hello. He doesn't laugh at my swooshy long johns or floppy high-tops. He just shoots a glance at Officer Borsch, then says through his teeth, "I can't believe I stuck up for you!"

Now I'm embarrassed *and* baffled. "What...what do you mean? Why are you so mad?"

He says, "As if you didn't know," then turns and marches off. With my skateboard.

And I try running after him, but I can only shuffle in my shoes, and there's no keeping up with him. I call, "Wait! Casey, wait!" but he's gone. *Gone* gone.

I turn, and there are Marissa, Dot, and Holly, in a huddle on the porch with their eyes cranked completely open while Officer Borsch squints at where Casey disappeared from view. He says, "What's that boy's name?"

"What's his…? Casey."

"Casey what?"

I snap, "I don't *know*…," because I don't, but even if I *did*, I probably wouldn't tell him. I mean, I've seen that look in Officer Borsch's eye before, and even though I had no idea why Casey was acting so schizo, I sure didn't want him tagged with a jaywalking citation. Or one for walking on the wrong side of the road. Or for riding around without a helmet.

Officer Borsch doesn't whip out his ticket book and pen, though, he just mutters, "Popular this morning, aren't you?" then clears his throat and says, "You were telling me about a gas can?"

But something's clicking in my brain, and I'm not really ready to go back to thinking about vanishing gas cans at the moment. "You said Wagonwheel Road? What 'mess' were you talking about?"

He studies me, then says, "The usual New Year's Eve blowout. We get complaints all the time, but this one involved minors in possession."

"Of alcohol?"

"Among other things."

"Was it at 6324?" I turn to Marissa and ask, "Is that right? 6324?"

She nods.

Officer Borsch says, "I don't have the exact address. I just learned about it this morning in briefing." He eyes me. "These friends of yours?"

"Not exactly. But it *is* important to me. How about a name?"

"I probably shouldn't say—though it'll be in tomorrow's paper. Maybe I could just confirm?"

For a second I just blink at him. I mean, this is Officer Borsch. King of Cannot. The Man Who Mentors Mules. Mr. Bobby-by-the-Book. And he's finding it in his heart to bend the rules. For me.

I hold my breath and say, "Briggs?"

He nods. "The Doctor and the Missus aren't going to be able to cry their way out of this one."

"Are you saying this has happened before?"

He scowls. "Let's just say that they have their hands full with that son of theirs."

"Which one? Karl? Taylor? *Ben?*"

"You seem to know the family better than I do. Why don't you tell me."

Looking at him, I could tell he wasn't about to volunteer. So I ripped through the possibilities in my mind. Ben was oldest, so it made sense that he'd had the *time* to get into trouble with the law. But he seemed a lot different from the other two. More responsible.

Taylor was only in the eighth grade, so how much trouble could he have gotten into yet?

Course I was in the seventh grade, so forget *that* theory.

Then there was Karl. He sure seemed like a hothead, and even though he was only in the tenth grade, he acted a lot older. Rougher.

But what bothered me about that wasn't Karl. It was Brandon. What was Brandon doing being best friends with a guy who smoked dope and drank and had, well, cabaña parties?

But my brain was far enough away from my heart to know more than I wanted it to. I looked at Officer Borsch and said, "Karl."

And what's Officer Borsch do?

He nods.

All of a sudden it hits me why Casey was so mad. I turn to Marissa and say, "Heather!"

"What about her?"

"She must be telling everyone I called the police!"

Officer Borsch says, "You *were* there?"

"For a little while, yeah. We went to get my skateboard back but…"

He frowns at me. "And you saw what was going on?"

"A little. We stayed way away from it, though."

He's still frowning. "Ever think maybe you *should've* called?"

Well, that clamps my kisser. And I stand there looking back and forth between Officer Borsch and my friends, wrestling with the thought of doing that. I mean, it never even occurred to me. Those people in Taylor's backyard were like adults to me. The boys *shaved*, and the girls were all, you know, primed and painted. And the fact that inside, Heather and Tenille were drinking, well, they were Heather and Tenille—there's nothing any *policeman's* going to be able to change about that.

Officer Borsch says, "Regardless. There's a lot of unhappy parents this morning, but at least none of them are making arrangements at the morgue. I'm more interested in that gas can. What do you say we take a ride over to the Huntley property and try to straighten this out."

I grin at him and say, "Um...Isn't that a little out of your jurisdiction?"

He sighs. "It seems, Samantha, that I'm picking up some of your bad habits."

I laugh and say, "Okay, but I have to get dressed first."

He eyes me. "That would be a very good idea."

So Marissa, Holly, Dot, and I run off, and when we're ready, we find him in his car, talking into his radio. He ten-fours and then blinks at us. "You're not *all* coming..."

I say, "Oh yes we are...!" and before he can argue, we've piled in for our first adventure of the New Year.

FIFTEEN

The world was at the Huntleys'. A fire-department Blazer, a police car, two fire-department pickup trucks, Dallas' motorcycle, and a silver Town Car that said SUPERSTAR REALTY on the back doors. Officer Borsch squeezes his cruiser alongside the Town Car and parks, half off the driveway.

"You girls stay put. I'm going to try to explain the situation to Mr. Huntley and see if he'll allow you to show me where you saw that can." He powers down the windows a few inches, then gets out and says, "Stay!" like we're a pack of dogs he doesn't want escaping.

We gawk out the windows for a while, but there's not much to see because everyone seems to be down at the cabin. So after a few minutes of talking about the police car and the gadgets all over it, Marissa and Dot start talking about Casey—how cute he is; how no guys they knew would go through all that trouble to try and deliver a skateboard; how I've got to straighten things out with him because no guy does what he did unless he *likes* you. And I do my best to change the subject back to who-do-you-suppose-burned-down-Mary's-cabin, but they're seriously tuned in to the Love Channel, and my remote control is just not working.

And pretty soon I'm on beyond arguing with them, so they start talking about me like I'm not even there. Then Marissa says, "Well, it sure beats having a crush on Brandon."

That turns my tuner. "What!?"

Marissa looks at me. "Sorry."

"Who says I have a crush on Brandon?"

"You don't have to *say* it."

"Marissa, he's in high school!"

She shrugs. "So?"

"So he's way too old for me!"

"C'mon, Sammy—if you can't tell us, who *can* you tell?"

Nobody. It was too stupid. It had always been too stupid. Which is why no matter what she said, no matter what she thought, I could not, *would* not have a crush on Brandon McKenze. "Can we talk about something else? You guys are making a monster out of a mouse."

"Squeak! Squeak!"

"Eeeek!!!"

I roll my eyes and say, "Oh, shut up," and before they can say anything back, there's a *tap-tap-tap* on the window.

We all whip around and there, peeking in at us with a little smile on her face, is Lucinda. She opens a door and says, "So glad you girls came by. Why don't you come out?"

I say, "We uh…we have direct orders not to."

"You do, do you?"

"Officer Borsch says someone complained about us being here."

"Well, I certainly didn't complain! I wonder who did?"

"Maybe your nephew?"

Lucinda frowns, but doesn't say a word.

Holly says, "Officer Borsch is trying to get permission to let us show him where we found a gas can last night, but he's taking a long time coming back, so I don't know if Kevin's going to let us or not."

Lucinda doesn't know anything about what's happened, so we have to tell the story all over again. And when we're done, she says, "Get out of the car."

"But—"

"Get out. I don't care what your police friend says, I don't care what my nephew says. This world is full of nitwits and leeches, and there are plenty of them assembled here today. They talk to me like I'm five years old, then pat my hand and walk away. They'd rather talk to someone who doesn't know a tree from a toadstool than take the time to gather some background to figure the situation out. I told 'em it was the Murdocks. I told 'em what Dorene and her ma said, but none of them seem to want to *listen*."

We scoot out of the car, but Dot says, "We're still going to be in a lot of trouble if Officer Borsch comes back and we're not here."

"Why?" Lucinda asks. "This is my property, and if I say you're welcome, you're welcome. I'll have to have a talk with Kevin when this tribe decides to leave, but for right now I want you to show me just where you found that can. If they won't get to the bottom of this, I will."

It's funny. I've always thought that the reason adults didn't pay attention to what I had to say was because I wasn't one of them. But here was the oldest person I'd ever met talking like she had the same problem, and it gave me a terrible thought: Maybe things *wouldn't* get better as I got older; maybe they'd only get worse.

We closed up the car and followed Lucinda down the dirt path to the cabin. And I don't know why, but the rubble looked even more depressing during the day than it had at night. Maybe black on black doesn't look so *dark,* I don't know, but in the bright light of day, what was left of Mary's cabin looked creepy. Wicked.

We stayed back for a minute, watching. Kevin was talking with a small man in a suit, and judging by Kevin's head shaking back and forth, the two of them were disagreeing about something. Then there was Officer Borsch, having a powwow with another policeman and two other men. Dallas was by himself, kind of kicking through the rubble, and you could tell he was thinking really hard about something. He sees us and waves, then comes over and keeps his voice down as he says to Lucinda, "Is there anything I can do? I feel so bad about this whole thing."

Lucinda nods. "I heard the fire chief talking about a bulldozer this morning. Whose idea was that?"

Dallas fiddles with the tusk on his necklace and says, "I…I'm not sure. You'll have to ask Kevin," but you can tell from the way he's looking down that the idea's Kevin's. All Kevin's.

"Why does he want to do that?"

Dallas scratches his forehead and sighs. "I think he thinks it'll make it easier on you."

"Well, it doesn't!"

He glances at us and says, "Uh, my understanding is Kevin's not wild about these kids being here…"

"He doesn't have to be wild about it, but he'd better get used to it." Then she tells him all about us finding the gas can and grumbles to him about nitwits and leeches.

He says something about her being too hard on people doing their jobs and then asks us to tell him about the gas can. So we do, and when we're all done, he says, "Are you sure it's not still down there? Maybe you just couldn't find it back in the dark?"

I say, "We searched," and Holly adds, "But maybe. We did get kinda spooked."

He says, "So let's have a look."

I say, "Um, maybe you can send that policeman over here first?"

"Which one?"

"The big one."

So Dallas interrupts Officer Borsch's powwow, and when he sees us standing underneath the tree, he marches over and says, "I thought I told you to stay…!"

I shrug. "I know, but Lucinda found us panting for air and let us out for a walk."

Lucinda puts out a hand. "Lucinda Huntley. Descendant of Mary Rose Huntley, the pioneer who built that cabin."

Officer Borsch barely shakes her hand. "You're better today, I see."

"I've composed myself, young man. That doesn't erase the tragedy. I intend to get to the bottom of this, and if you're going to stand there and tell me why things *can't* be done, maybe you should just step aside."

The slits Officer Borsch sports for eyes were open wider than I'd ever seen them. He turns to me and says, "Just exactly what have you been telling this woman?"

"Nothing! Really!"

Lucinda says, "They've told me about the gas can, and what I don't understand is why someone isn't scouring that ravine now, looking for pyroglyphics or pyrotechnics or whatever you people call fire starters."

"Your nephew, ma'am, is the reason. He doesn't seem to want to be interrupted, and I didn't think it wise to proceed without him."

Lucinda gives Kevin a disgusted look and says, "Well, this property is still mine, and I want that ravine searched."

"Okay then." Officer Borsch turns to me and says, "Sammy—was it metal or plastic?"

"Metal."

"New? Old? Describe it the best you can."

"It seemed pretty new. It was rectangular, red and silver, and had GASOLINE printed across it. On a diagonal."

"Did it have a spout?"

"No spout and no lid."

"Okay. Show me the area where you remember seeing it."

Dallas eyes Kevin and says, "You still might want to get Kevin to agree…it would make things easier in the long run."

Officer Borsch nods and leads the way over to Kevin. He interrupts with, "Excuse me, Mr. Huntley…"

Kevin looks at Officer Borsch, then Lucinda and the

rest of us. And before he can start about how come we're trespassing on his property, Officer Borsch says, "Your aunt has granted these girls permission to point out the area where they say they discovered a gas can last night. Do you mind if we conduct a search?"

To everyone's surprise, Kevin says, "That's fine."

He goes back to talking with Slick Suit, and the rest of us shrug and head for the ravine. I spot the rock we'd left as a marker, then point down the hill. "Right down there. About halfway."

The ravine is covered with oak leaves, and as you step down, you sink past your ankle, sometimes clear up to your shin. Officer Borsch takes a few steps and says, "How did you ever see it, at night, in all of this mulch?"

"Penny showed it to us."

He stops. "Penny? Who's Penny?"

"Lucinda's pig."

The minute it came out of my mouth I knew it sounded ridiculous. Officer Borsch bows his head, and his voice is hoarse as he says, "Tell me you didn't just say pig."

Lucinda says, "She's a very smart pig, young man." She turns to Dallas. "Isn't that so?"

Dallas shrugs and nods, so Officer Borsch sighs and says, "I'm sure she is, ma'am." Then he looks at me. "Okay, Sammy. I'm going to rewind. I'm going to try to forget that I ever asked, okay?"

"Yes sir."

"You found the can right down here. About halfway?"

"That's right."

He crunches his way down the ravine muttering, "Our

next witness? Yes, Your Honor. We call Penny the Pig to the stand..."

So we watch Officer Borsch search the area, first with his hands, then by poking a stick into the mulch all around him. And while he's searching, Kevin comes over to watch.

Lucinda asks him, "Who *is* that man you were talking to?"

Kevin's quiet for a minute, just watching. But he knows Lucinda's got both eyes on him, so finally he says, "He's a real-estate agent. There's been an offer on the property."

"*Our* property?"

"That's right."

"But it's not on the market!"

He shakes his head and sighs. "They've been interested for a while. They approached me about six months ago—"

Lucinda interrupts him. "Why didn't you ever say anything?"

"You were ill, remember? And I knew there was no sense in discussing it. Not with Mary's cabin standing."

"You told them that?"

"Well, sure. I explained how important the property was to you and that you wouldn't be interested in selling it. But Aunt Lucinda, now that the cabin's gone, there's nothing left tying us here. I know you're on this crusade to prove that the Murdocks burned the place down, but even if they did, it won't bring the cabin back." Very quietly he adds, "If you ask me, this whole thing might be a blessing."

"How can you *say* that?"

"Aunt Lucinda, you've been living in the past for years.

Decades! I admire Mary, but she's gone. Long gone. Don't you ever want to get out of this place and enjoy what's left of your life?"

She looks up at him and says, "Are you speaking about me or about you?"

He pushes back the brim of his hat and sighs. "If you look at the financial reality of it, we have to do *something*. The crops have been miserable for the past three years, and—"

"But this vineyard produced the finest grapes in the county—perhaps the state!"

"Aunt Lucinda, again, you're living in the past."

Lucinda crosses her arms, thinking. Then she turns to Kevin and says, "It must be a pretty penny they're offering."

He whispers, "Half a million."

Lucinda scowls. "And where do *we* go? To the city? Or are you planning to just check me in to an old folks' home and be done with it?"

"You know I would never do that! The reason I've held on so long is because of you."

"Hmmm," she says. "What do real-estate agents get these days? Ten percent? Fifteen? Tidy little commission, don't you think?"

Kevin looks down. "I told him we weren't interested."

"And yet he was here. On New Year's Day, no less."

"Like I said, I told him we weren't interested."

Lucinda gives him a little smile. "But he knows you're lying. Leeches can always find the soft spot."

"It's business, Lucinda."

She snickers. "And a very profitable one for him—if he can convince us to sell."

Just then Officer Borsch comes up the hill saying, "Well, I find nothing down there. If there was a can, it's gone now."

"What about the cap?" I ask. "Can't we use giant sieves or something and sift through the leaves for it?"

Officer Borsch looks at me like I'm talking about pigs again. He comes up the rest of the way, stomps leaves off his boots, and says, "Even if we did find it, we couldn't get any prints off of it. By now they're completely dusted over."

"So, it's just our word that something was there."

Officer Borsch shakes his head. "No, the fire marshal has confirmed that an accelerant was used. The cabin was definitely set on fire."

"How in the world can they tell that?" Kevin asks, looking at the rubble.

"From the burn pattern of the timbers."

"But there's nothing left of them!"

Officer Borsch says, "There's enough."

Lucinda throws her hands in the air. "So what are you waiting for? Go arrest those devils!"

Officer Borsch stares at her. "What devils?"

"The Murdocks!"

"Ma'am, with all due respect, I can't go around arresting people without just cause."

While Lucinda's telling him a thing or two about just cause, I'm thinking that maybe I didn't know the Murdocks, but their torching Mary's cabin just to get back at Lucinda seemed pretty extreme. And that the more I learned, the more it felt like this situation went deeper than revenge.

Miles deeper.

SIXTEEN

Penny is definitely not a proud pig. I mean, it's one thing to nudge *me* from behind—it's quite another to do it to Officer Borsch.

I don't think she was trying to get him to quit arguing with Lucinda about "ancient history" and "just cause" as much as she was just sniffing him out, but she might as well have goosed him for all the noise he made. He jumps back, crying, "Hey! Heeeeey! Get away from me!"

Penny snorts after him, twitching her snout around in the air.

"You hear me? Get away!"

I grab her collar to hold her back, but she is two hundred pounds of highly motivated pork, and I'm not having much of an effect. I practically get on her and go for a ride, but still, she's not stopping.

Then this giggle consumes me. Completely. I can't stop it any more than I can stop Penny. And it's not because I think the way Officer Borsch is acting is funny. Try being attacked by a runaway pig sometime—it's scary! No, it's because I realize that Penny's in love. L-O-V-E, love.

Now a thought like that can put you in stitches, and a thought like that can make you completely useless. At least that's what it did to me—I just fell over laughing.

And while Penny's chasing Officer Borsch around a giant oak tree, everyone else starts busting up, too.

Officer Borsch yells at us, "It's not funny! Get this thing away from me!" and as he's playing ring-around-the-oak-tree with Penny it dawns on him that the other police and the fire people are watching him and starting to laugh, too. That's when he decides that the only way to stop Penny is to do the job himself.

All of a sudden he quits running, spins around, and plants himself like he's ready to wrestle a bear. Penny stops, all right, then stands in front of him, snorting and sniffing and twitching her tail.

He takes a step back.

She takes a step forward.

He tries taking a step to the side.

She takes one, too.

He takes a step *forward*.

She stays put.

Lucinda whispers, "I wonder what's gotten into her!"

Now I'm not going to start talking about Oinkers in Love; somehow I don't think Lucinda would approve. I just ask, "Will she come if you call her?"

"Usually. Although she can be quite stubborn."

We all look at her like, Well?

She says, "Oh! Oh, I suppose you're right," then tries calling off her pig. "Penny! Come here, girl!"

Penny rolls an eye around to Lucinda, then inches closer to Officer Borsch.

"Penny, you come here this instant!"

Penny snorts and twitches her tail.

157

Lucinda marches up to her and wags a bony finger, saying, "Penny, mind!"

If a pig can grumble, then that's exactly what Penny did. But she came away from Officer Borsch without so much as a yank of the collar. And when she'd followed Lucinda a safe distance away, Officer Borsch lets out a deep breath, wipes his forehead, and grumbles something about cursed country living and being *way* out of his jurisdiction. Then he calls, "Can you girls make it back on your own all right? I need to wrap things up and get back to town."

We wave him off, saying we're fine, and Lucinda calls, "So what's going to happen? Are you going to arrest those Murdocks?"

Officer Borsch says, "I'm sure we'll be sending someone over to question them," then has a quick chat with the other uniforms before skating out of there.

Dallas lets out a sigh. "Well, I'm afraid that's that."

Lucinda says, "What do you mean?"

He shrugs. "I know you want them to go arrest that whole clan, but it's not going to happen. They've got no evidence, they've got no proof…"

All this time, Kevin's been standing to the side, listening. But when he hears that, he steps closer and says, "Dallas is right. Nobody understands the historical value of it, Aunt Lucinda. To them it was just an old shack."

Lucinda is quiet for a minute, looking from Dallas to Kevin. Finally, she sighs and says, "I think I'll go in and rest," but I can tell by the look in her eye that she's not tired. Not in the least.

The four of us follow Lucinda back to the house while Kevin and Dallas stand around talking. And after we're about halfway there I say, "Lucinda, I read Mary's diary last night…"

She stops and looks at me carefully. "And?"

"And it's the most amazing thing I've ever read."

She gives me a little smile. "Thank you."

"I'm serious."

Dot says, "Yeah, I found her this morning buried in her sleeping bag with the flashlight on and the diary open, and over breakfast that's all she talked about."

Lucinda takes my hand and says, "You really do understand, then."

I nod.

She searches my face. "Did the last page make any sense to you? Any sense at all?"

"The riddle about the gold?"

"Yes. Did it?"

"It keeps playing through my head, but no. The only thing I can think for the part…how's it go? *Where the ridge meets the rock and the rock meets the ground…*"

Lucinda nods, "Yes, that's right."

"The only thing that makes sense to me is that there must be someplace along the ravine where rocks go from the edge of it clear down to the bottom. Is there someplace like that?"

"I've looked. Kevin's looked. Dallas has looked. Because that's what we all thought. And there are places like that, but…nothing."

"*The box is shallow, black and crowned…* That must be

the box the gold is in? Like it has a crown stamped on it or something?"

Lucinda shrugs. "I don't know. Kevin's suggested maybe it was jeweled, but I don't know where Mary would've gotten *jewels*."

"Maybe it's decorated with pretty stones?"

Lucinda frowns. "My hunch is it has nothing to do with jewels or stones, but what then?"

"How's the rest go? *Not far in, left and high, gold and silver, warm inside?*"

"That's right."

"All I see is rocks in the sun, getting hot. That's the picture that keeps popping into my head."

She sighs, "It's no use. That's what the rest of us have come up with." Her face gets all stormy, and she starts marching again, only this time faster. "It feels like I've lost everything. Or will, soon enough. And if I can't do anything else about it, at least I can see to it that their actions don't go unavenged."

I had no idea what she had in mind, but the jut of her jaw and the tone of her voice put me in a bit of a panic. "Lucinda, wait! What are you talking about? The Murdocks? C'mon, they're...they're like mosquitoes. They buzz and they bite and they leave itchy spots, but they're...you know...just pests!" She was shuffling along like a locomotive, gathering speed. "Lucinda, wait! What are you going to do? You can't—"

"I'm tired of people telling me what I cannot do, what I did not see, and what I should not believe! Others seem to do what they pretty well please, and I haven't got enough time left to worry about the consequences."

"But what if it *wasn't* the Murdocks. What if—"

"Ha!" she says, then turns before going up the steps to a side door. "This stinks of Murdock if anything ever did. It's sneaky and mean-spirited and there's the stench of money in the air." We follow her up the steps, but she's not about to let us in. She says, "I've enjoyed your company, but if you'll excuse me, I've got matters to attend to," and lets the screen door slam behind her.

I look at the others and say, "What are we going to *do*?"

We stand at the base of the steps trying to decide. Nobody wants to talk to Kevin—not with the way we'd been banned from the property. Officer Borsch was already gone, and when Dot brought up talking with the other policemen, Holly pointed to the vacant driveway and said, "Too late for that."

It was too late to talk to Dallas, too. His motorcycle was gone. Then Dot says, "We could always go talk to the Murdocks ourselves."

I snicker and say, "We could go swimming with barracudas, too."

Holly says to Dot, "You can't be *serious*?"

"Sure. Why not?"

I ask her, "What are you planning to *say*?"

"I don't know—maybe 'Hi. We're here because Lucinda Huntley is real upset about the cabin being burned down and we're afraid she's going to do something drastic.'"

"She'd kill us!"

Dot looks me square in the eye. "It's better than her killing someone for real."

Maybe I should have laughed, but I couldn't. I mean, sure, it seemed kind of far-fetched that an old woman, bent like a cane, would haul off and blast someone with a shotgun, but the more I got to know Lucinda, the more I believed that she actually might.

So we hiked up the hill and around the bend to the Murdocks'. And when we got to their driveway, Marissa said, "Are we sure we want to do this?"

We weren't. So we hovered there, trying to decide exactly what to say. Then I noticed something. Off the driveway on the gravel, hidden behind a hedge, was a car. And even though I could only see the taillights and the back bumper, I was pretty sure it was the Town Car that had just been at the Huntleys'. I point and say, "Look! Right up there...behind the hedge. Is that the realtor's car?"

We tiptoe up, and sure enough, there's the SUPERSTAR REALTY placard on the side. Holly says, "Do you think the *Murdocks* are trying to buy the Huntley property?"

I look at her and mutter, "Well, he's hiding something. Why else would he park here?" Then I get a tingle along my spine. "Do you remember the first time we met Lucinda?"

Holly says, "On the road with Dot's dad?"

"Yeah. Do you remember the car that came by?"

"Yeah...It was silver, too, but Sammy, it didn't say SUPERSTAR REALTY on it. I would've remembered that."

I walk up to the car, pinch the corner of the placard and pull, and there I am with a giant sign magnet in my hand. "What about now? Same car?"

They all shake their heads and say, "Wow," and "Maybe," and "I remember the windows were tinted just like those but…"

Then Marissa says, "So let's say it was. What are you saying? That *he* burned the place down?"

"I don't know! But that's pretty suspicious, don't you think?"

"So what do you want to do?"

I think about it a minute. "Let's just wait it out."

"You mean just hang out here until he comes out? Or until Lucinda shows up?"

"Either one."

Marissa whispers, "Guys, I don't see what good any of this is going to do. If you think the SuperStar guy is involved, why wait around here? And if you go up and tell the Murdocks to watch out for Lucinda, they'll just laugh at you. And if Lucinda really does come marching up here with a gun, she's crazy, and I'm not going to try to wrestle a gun from her."

I shrug and say, "It's better than letting her blow someone away. I mean, I don't want her killing anyone, and I sure don't want her going to jail."

We were all quiet for a minute, thinking about little Lucinda sitting in a jail cell, waiting to be arraigned so she could explain about wagon trains and Murdocks and the ghost of Moustache Mary. No judge would understand it. No judge would even believe her. They'd give her a sad little look and know, just *know*, that she was demented.

I whisper, "You guys can go, but I want to stick around for a while."

Marissa says, "What are you going to do, just sit here and wait?"

I nod and say, "Really, why don't you guys go back to Dot's? I'll be there in a little while."

Holly puts her hands in her pockets. "If you're staying, I'm staying."

Dot and Marissa look at each other, then shrug and say, "We'll wait, too."

We all take cover beside some bushes near the house, which is a great spot because we can see the front door and the driveway, but we're pretty well concealed from view. So we sit there, whispering back and forth about the Town Car and the Huntleys, the Murdocks and the gas can, but after a while I start getting antsy. And since there are perfectly good windows just begging to get peeked into, I decide to sneak over and see what I can see.

Marissa shakes her head, saying, "There she goes," and Dot whispers, "Sammy...Sammy, no! Can't you just sit still?"

I put my finger to my mouth and then grin and shake my head.

Dot whispers, "You're going to get us into trou-ble...!" so I whisper right back, "No I'm no-ot...!"

She rolls her eyes, and she and Marissa stay put, but Holly sneaks over to my side and we both inch up and peek in the first window.

Now there are curtains—heavy green velvet ones—but they're swagged to the side, and the lace panel that falls between them is easy to see through. Holly whispers, "Whoa...! That's some sitting room!"

The room itself isn't very big, but it's outfitted like they're expecting Napoleon. There's a crystal chandelier, marble columns with busts on top, glass coffee and end tables held up by brass lions…the room's just packed with glass, brass, and marble.

When we get tired of gawking at that room, we hunch down and scoot over to the next one. Same story. Only this room's much bigger and has gadgets Napoleon never dreamed of. There's a huge television screen, looking like a black hole on the far end of a galaxy of lights. There are speakers like giant asteroids suspended from the ceiling, and behind some smoky black doors is a stack of stereo gear with little green and red lights glowing like hieroglyphics from outer space.

I whisper to Marissa, "You are really missing out. This place makes your little mansion look like a flophouse!"

Marissa couldn't resist that. She and Dot sneak over to the first window, and when their eyes are all good and bugged out, I say, "Told you."

They join us at the second window, and when Marissa sees what's inside, she lets out a low whistle and says, "Wow!"

And it struck me as odd that the Murdocks had so much and the Huntleys had so little, when they'd started out the same way, scrapping for food and water on a wagon train.

Holly ducks away from the third window and faces us with a finger tapping away at her lips.

We scurry over and she whispers, "They're in there."

"Who?"

"I don't know. A bunch of people."

Marissa and Dot stay low, but Holly and I inch our noses up until we can see inside. There's a chubby man with slicked-back hair and cowboy boots, kicking back in an oversize leather chair, smoking a cigar, and he seems amused, puffing away with his feet propped up. Then there's Dorene and Ma looking like dandelions trying to pass as daffodils. They've got their fists clamped around the stems of champagne glasses, and they're plopped down on either end of a suede couch with their knee-high nylons sagged down to their ankles.

The real-estate guy is there, too, and he's sitting in an oversize leather chair, but his feet aren't propped up like Chubby's. They're flat on the floor, and he's using his briefcase as a lap table for his champagne glass, looking kind of uncomfortable.

Dot tugs on me and says, "What do you see? What's going on in there?"

So I crouch down and tell them, and before you know it, Marissa and Dot have their noses on the sill, too.

Holly whispers, "The SuperStar guy keeps looking at his watch. Do you think they're waiting for something?"

Just then the butler appears in the doorway. His eyes are still at half-mast, and his nose is looking even worse than it had the day before. He puts his fingertips together at his waist, says a few words, then makes a stiff little bow and disappears.

Thirty seconds later, Snout St. Helens returns, only this time he's got company. Two men. And they could've passed for Secret Service, only they weren't wearing sunglasses, and their ties poufed a little too much at the knots. One of them's got a briefcase, and the other one is carrying blue-prints.

The Snout offers them champagne, then goes around refilling everyone else's glass before leaving the room.

Dot says, "Who are *those* guys?"

Marissa checks over her shoulder and whispers, "And where'd they come from? I didn't hear them drive up."

She had a point. We had wandered pretty far from the drive, and if we were there to intercept Lucinda, we were doing a pretty miserable job. But I couldn't leave, either. Not with them in there unrolling blueprints.

It's like Holly read my mind. "You want me to keep watch at the drive?"

I nod, so she and Dot scurry off while Marissa and I watch the Suits point and talk and turn through the blue-prints. Finally, Marissa says, "Those guys can't be realtors. Do you think maybe they're developers?"

"Maybe..."

Just then Snout St. Helens reappears and makes a grand swooping motion with one arm as he announces another visitor.

And both of our jaws drop, because this time it's some-one we *do* know.

SEVENTEEN

Marissa gasps, "What's *Kevin* doing in there?"

Holly and Dot come scurrying back as we watch Chubby offer Kevin a cigar. Holly's all out of breath, saying, "Is he in there already?"

I nod and scowl. "Take a look."

Even though Kevin Huntley looked out of place, holding his dirty hat in his hand, wearing dusty clothes and a rope belt, he didn't look uncomfortable. Like he'd been there before. Many times before.

Holly and Dot were still trying to catch their breath. Dot says, "God, he almost saw us. We hid behind the other car, but it was close!"

Holly adds, "Boy, is Lucinda going to be upset when she finds out about this."

I shake my head. "She's gonna *die*."

Then Holly says, "Sammy, there are more blueprints in their car. We spotted them on the back seat."

I turn to look at her. "Really?"

"I don't know that they're the same ones...why would they bring more than one set?"

Marissa whispers, "Oh, I wouldn't be surprised if they were duplicates. Developers always make a bunch of copies. They have a set, they give a set to the owner, one to the contractor, and then all the subcontractors, too..."

I didn't wait around to find out *how* Marissa knew this. She's Yolanda's daughter, after all—she knows about stuff like contractors and subcontractors. Instead, I scampered over to the Suits' car and tried the driver's door. Then I ran around and tried the passenger door. The others are right behind me, whispering, "Sammy, you can't just *take* them!"

"I only want to look at them. I'll put them back..."

The doors are locked, but there *is* another way in. Holly and I both eye the sunroof, which is wide open. She grins and says, "Go for it!"

I use the door handle like a ladder and climb up. And in no time I've dived in and pulled out the blueprints. We hightail it out of view, then duck beneath an old oak tree and roll out the blueprints, right there in the dirt.

In big blue letters down one side it says CROMWELL AND YATES, DEVELOPMENT ASSOCIATES, and across the top it reads GOLD HILLS COUNTRY CLUB. We study the plans for a minute, then Marissa points to the blueprints, saying, "This over here must be the Murdocks' property, this right here is the ravine, this little square is Mary's cabin, and this bigger square must be Lucinda's house. The Huntley property stops right here, and this...well, they must already own this."

Dot adds, "Unless ACQUIRED is a very weird family name."

After we spend some time soaking it all in, we turn the page and there's an artist's sketch of the development being planned, complete with country club estates, golf course, swimming pools, tennis courts, a giant clubhouse, a restaurant, and a bar.

Dot whispers, "Wow!" and we all agree, this is one big-bucks project.

Then Marissa says, "The whole thing's gated—look at that entrance!"

Holly says, "Doesn't that road run right over Mary's cabin?"

I nod. "Exactly. And from the way they've laid out the golf course, and the ravine being where it is, this is the only place they can really use as an entrance."

Holly adds, "And they *have* to have the Huntley property to tie the other two properties together."

Marissa says, "Plans like this cost a lot to have done. And I don't think anyone would go through all the time and trouble to draft them up unless they were pretty darn sure they were going to be able to get the Huntleys to sell."

"And you know *Lucinda* never gave them that impression."

After we talk it out, Holly rolls up the blueprints and says, "We can't put these back. We have to show them to Lucinda."

We all agree, and hurry off Murdock property and down the road, diving out of view every time a car comes along, and when we get to the break in the fence, we squeeze through to take the back way in. We follow the path a little ways, but then Marissa says, "Let's cut through the vineyard, okay? That cabin gives me the creeps."

So we turn before the toolshed and make our way through the vineyard. When we get to the Huntleys' house, we ring the bell and knock, then ring and knock some more. Finally, the door swings open, and there's Lucinda, looking an inch shorter and ten years older. "Girls," she says. "How nice."

We say our hellos, then Holly asks, "Can we come in? We have something we have to show you."

She comes out, instead. "Have you seen my Penny?" She inspects a dish of vegetable parts on the porch and says, "I put lunch out for her, but she hasn't come. I wonder where she could be?" She gives us half a smile and asks, "You wanted to show me something?"

Dot starts rolling open the blueprints right there on the porch, but the rest of us are kind of checking over our shoulders, worried that Kevin might be back soon.

Holly says, "Can we maybe do this inside?"

So Lucinda lets us in, but the minute the door's closed, she says, "If my nephew happens home, I'll have to have you sneak out the back."

"You think he'd be mad if we were here?" I ask.

"I suspect so. He swears he's not the one who called the police about you, but he's been very testy about... about everything." She lets out a long, tired sigh. "He just doesn't understand, and I'm afraid I don't understand him. It seems that money—or the lack of it—can turn babes into beasts." She shakes her head and says, "It's a shift in priorities, I suppose. I just don't need what he wants. All I want is my family, and my family is Kevin."

At that moment I wanted to ditch the blueprints. Tear

them up. Burn them. I wanted to *help* Lucinda, not hurt her. But tearing up the blueprints wouldn't make the *plans* go away; wouldn't stop the avalanche that was sliding straight for Lucinda's heart.

So I take a deep breath and say, "Lucinda, we stole something."

"Oh?"

"These."

"Blueprints?" She seemed puzzled. Like we were offering spinach for breakfast.

Dot helps her roll them out, and Marissa explains what's what. Halfway through, Lucinda says, "Oh my Lord, are you telling me that this is an entire development planned without my consent?"

Holly says, "That's what it looks like to us."

"But who...?"

"Cromwell and Associates Developers, that SuperStar Realty creep, the Murdocks and..." I just couldn't say it.

She blinks at us, then turns back to the blueprints. "But surely they wouldn't have done this unless they had some assurance that we'd sell them the property!"

We all nod at her as the only possible answer sinks in. "Kevin?" she gasps. "In cahoots with the Murdocks?"

I whisper, "He's over there right now."

You'd think that news like that would make Lucinda shrink another inch. Maybe make her break down and cry. But instead, she squares her shoulders the best she can, takes the blueprints to the kitchen table, and says, "I want to be able to read these myself. My glasses are up on my nightstand—would one of you be so kind?"

I said, "Sure," and took the steps by two, racing to her room. And I would've just grabbed the glasses and charged back down the stairs, only as I'm turning to go, that picture of Kevin with a bunch of grape crates in the back of a pickup catches my eye. And I do a double-take because all of a sudden I realize that the truck under all those grapes is one I've seen before. I pick up the photo for a better look, and sure enough. It's primer-gray with wide wheels and huge sideview mirrors.

And the last time I'd seen it, it was sitting in the Briggs brothers' driveway.

EIGHTEEN

I grabbed the photograph *and* the glasses. And when I got downstairs, I handed them both to Lucinda and said, "What can you tell me about the truck in this picture?"

She put on her glasses but still held the picture out at arm's length. "The *truck*? I don't know. Kevin owned it for a number of years—used it for hauling. He gave it to Dallas to square off back wages."

"Does...does Dallas still own it?"

"Oh no. I think he sold it to a friend. I've only ever seen him drive his motorcycle." She smiles at the photograph and says, "Those were better times. Look at that bounty of grapes! And the smile on Kevin's face."

I looked, but I wasn't seeing the grapes or Kevin's face. I was seeing the truck. It was the Briggses' truck. I was positive. And in my mind the trouble with Huntleys and Murdocks had suddenly been pushed aside—not by thoughts of Ben or Karl or the way Taylor had held my skateboard hostage, but by thoughts of who I'd been with under that truck.

And the more I thought about Casey, the more I knew that Marissa was right. He had gone way out on a limb for me. He had stuck up for me and tried to help me, and he'd been nice. Really nice. And even though he was an eighth grader, he didn't make me feel like a little kid the way Taylor did. He treated me like I was his equal. His friend.

And being around him hadn't felt weird or awkward. I hadn't worried about what to say or do. I'd just been me, and he'd *liked* me.

I don't know how I wound up with the picture back in my hands. Everyone else had turned to look at the blueprints, but there I was, hypnotized by a picture of an old truck.

Marissa whispers, "Sammy? Sammy, are you all right?"

I wasn't. I was feeling very strange. Almost dizzy. And my heart was doing weird things, skipping around, like it wasn't really sure where it should go.

"Sammy?"

It barely came out a whisper. "He trusted me. And now he believes Heather. *Heather.*"

"What are you talking about?"

I look up at her. "I've got to straighten things out with Casey."

"What?"

I put down the picture and said it louder. "I've got to go straighten things out with Casey."

Marissa's eyebrows went way up. "Seriously?"

Holly turns to us and says, "What are you guys talking about?"

Marissa smiles and says, "She wants to go straighten things out with Casey."

Holly looks at me and then at Lucinda poring over the blueprints. *"Now?"*

I'd never felt like this before. Murdocks and Huntleys, developers and real-estate snakes—they could wait. But somehow, straightening things out with Casey couldn't.

Lucinda takes one look at me and says, "You go on. I need some time to think this through on my own, anyway."

At least Holly's still got her wits about her. She asks Lucinda, "What are you going to do when Kevin comes back?"

"I don't know. Kevin's thumbprint may be on this, but he's still my kin. Nothing can ever change that."

We left her to study the Gold Hills Country Club blueprints, and as we made our way out to the road, Marissa starts right in quizzing me about Casey: What am I going to *say* to him? Does this mean I *like* him? Do I want her to come *with* me...?

Then Holly cuts in with stuff like: You don't even know where he *lives,* and, How are you going to *get* there? and, Why don't you just find out his number and *call* him?

And it's funny—normally I would've told them to be quiet so I could figure it all out—*plan* it all out—but for some reason I just kept on walking, saying stuff like, I don't know, and, I'll see.

Finally, I ask Dot, "Have you heard of Golden Oak Circle?"

"No...why? Is that the street he lives on?"

A grin escapes as I say, "Yup. 782," but I catch it right away and lock it back up. "Golden Oak sounds like it would be around here somewhere."

Marissa eyes me. "How do you know he lives there?"

I shrug and say, "He told me."

"And you *remembered*."

Marissa's switching over to the Love Channel fast, but Dot's got a different frequency in mind: the Food Channel. She says, "Why are we walking so slow? Isn't anyone but me starving?"

So we speed it up, and when we get to the DeVrieses', the rest of the family has already eaten, so we chow down on leftover pumpernickel and cheese sandwiches. And while Nibbles is vacuuming up leftovers, Mrs. DeVries digs up a map so I can figure out where Golden Oak Circle is.

It turned out to be right in Pioneer Village, four streets down from Wagonwheel Road. And even though I felt kind of queasy, heading off on my own, I knew I couldn't arrive at Casey's house with an entourage of friends. It'd be too...you know, fourth grade.

But by the time I got to the main road, I was asking myself some of the same things Marissa had asked me: What was I going to say? What if he didn't listen? Why was I doing this, anyway? And the more my brain bombarded me with questions, the more I knew I had to shut them off or I'd turn around. So I cranked the bike pedals as hard as I could and hauled my way up to Pioneer Village.

By the time I'd passed by Wagonwheel Road, I was so out of breath my brain couldn't think about anything but oxygen. Then I spotted Golden Oak Circle, and there came those questions again. And at the top of the list, repeating itself again and again, was, What am I *doing* here?

But there I was. And after hanging across the street from 782 for a few minutes, I crossed over, parked Hudson's bike on the grass, and went up to the front door.

And when I punched the button and heard the doorbell ringing inside, well, I almost turned around and ran. Why did I care what Casey thought? So he thought I called the cops. So what?

Then the door swings open, and there he is, right in front of me.

I look down and blurt out, "I had nothing to do with calling the police. Maybe I *should've*, but I didn't. And the reason there was a policeman over at Dot's when you came by was because somebody burned down this old pioneer cabin up the road from Dot's, and we happened to find the gas can."

For a minute, he doesn't say anything. Then he asks, "Are you talking about the Huntley cabin?"

"That's right."

"My dad was talking about that this morning." He came out onto the porch and closed the door. "But you're saying someone *lit* it?"

"Uh-huh." So I told him all about the cabin and Lucinda and the Murdocks hating the Huntleys, and how we'd figured out that there were developers dying to turn that whole area of land into some ritzy country club estates. And I don't even remember doing it, but somewhere in the middle of me talking, we wind up sitting down on the porch steps, right next to each other.

Now while I'm talking, I'm looking at my high-tops or the grass in the yard, or the phone lines stretching across the street. I'm sure not looking at him. Oh, I glance at him every now and then, but right away I go back to looking at something else.

Trouble is, *he's* looking at *me*. And I keep forgetting parts of the story and having to put them in later because I'm distracted by the fact that my cheeks are on fire and I have no idea what in the world he's *thinking*.

Finally, I say, "So there. That's the story. And you probably don't even care, but I don't like it when people accuse me of things I didn't do. And really, this whole thing is my fault because I shouldn't have been at the party in the first place."

"It was fine that you were there."

"No, no it wasn't. Those people may be your friends—or friends of your friend's brother—but they're not my friends, and they're not people I want to know or hang around."

"Oh come on, they're not that bad. I've been friends with Taylor since we were six. Jake, too. They can both get kind of crazed, but you just flow with them and say no thanks when you want to say no thanks."

"So what if where they're flowing is not where you want to go? What if where they're flowing's going to pull you down and drown you?"

He shrugs. "Then you just bail."

"What if you can't? What if you don't even see where you're going until it's too late? What if—"

He grabs my shoulders and shakes me a little. "Hey, take it easy! Everyone's fine. Why are you being so intense?"

Now I couldn't answer that. But something about the whole situation bothered me. Really bothered me. I mean, if Casey treated me like Taylor did—or even Jake, or Heather or Tenille for that matter—I probably wouldn't give it another thought. But he didn't treat me like his friends did. And he didn't act like them, either. So what was he doing, being part of the pack?

And I was about to ask him if he was friends with Taylor and Jake because he'd been friends with them for so long, or because he still really liked them, but before I could he gives me a little smile and says, "And thanks for the story, but I already knew you didn't call the cops."

"You...you did?"

He nods. "Taylor called about an hour ago and said they found out that their neighbors complained. Disturbance of the peace. And everything would've been cool, except Karl got mouthy and pretty soon the whole party got busted. The real problem is, the cops found Karl's stash of meth."

"Meth? What's that?"

"Oh, you know. Speed. Crank."

I stared at him. "No, I *don't* know."

"Oh. Well, you know what cocaine is, right?"

"Yeah, I guess so."

"Well, meth—methamphetamine—is kind of a cheap cocaine."

"Have...have you ever tried it?"

He laughs, "No!"

"So how do you know all this stuff?"

He kind of shrugs and says, "I don't know. You pick it up. Ben used to be seriously into meth, and Karl started pinching from him. Now Ben's like born again and thinks meth's a tool of the devil. The point is Karl tried meth in the first place because he saw Ben doing it." He eyes me and says, "All this is according to Taylor and Karl—I never actually witnessed any of this myself, so don't go spouting it as gospel."

I nod, but don't say a word.

"Anyway, after you guys left, Ben came back and caught *Taylor* snorting meth and he lost it. Absolutely raged. And the shouting's what set the neighbors off."

I sat there, stunned. I mean, sure, I know there are kids at school who smoke and drink beer, and I've heard rumors about ones who smoke more than cigarettes, but I don't actually *know* them. They're always people that *other* people know.

Finally, I whisper, "Doesn't it bother you that Taylor did that?"

He nods and looks down. "Yeah, actually it does. But it's not like he's a drug addict or something. I mean, it was his first time—he just *tried* it."

"But according to you, Ben used to be seriously into the stuff. Like, he was addicted, right?"

Casey shrugs. "Yeah. I guess so."

"So he would know. Better than you, better than me, better than his parents or Taylor or even the *police*, why his little brother shouldn't even *try* it, right?"

"Yeah. But Sammy, c'mon. He didn't have to lose it like that. Karl and Taylor think he's a total hypocrite and they're blaming everything on him. And now Karl, at least, is going to have some kind of a police record."

He stands and puts a hand out to help me up. "I also can't see bailing on Taylor and Jake as friends—I've known them too long. Besides, it would be weird not hanging with them. We're like, tight." He's still got my hand as he says, "You want to come in for something to drink?"

"I um…I really should get back to Dot's."

"How long's it take to get something to drink? Besides, you have to come in for a minute. I've got your skateboard to give you."

So I let him guide me inside. Through a foyer, past the living room and its half-brown Christmas tree, into the dining room. And I'd barely sat down on one of the breakfast bar stools when the refrigerator closes and my heart stops mid-beat because standing there with a jug of orange juice in her hand is Heather Acosta.

NINETEEN

I felt like I was hallucinating. But even in mangled hair and an oversize T-shirt, even with puffy eyes and saggy socks, there was no mistaking the Rabid Redhead.

My mind just exploded with explanations—It was a trap. A cruel joke. Heather was his girlfriend. Heather had gotten so drunk she'd lost her way home...You name it, I thought it.

The only thing I *didn't* think—because I couldn't even imagine it—was the truth.

Heather stands there with her fist wrapped around the orange juice jug, looking back and forth between Casey and me. Finally, she says, "My brother and the Narc. How sweet."

I felt like she'd slugged me in the stomach. Her *brother*? And as I'm gasping for air, I'm telling myself that it *can't* be. I mean, I'd been to Heather's house before. I knew where she lived, and it sure wasn't here!

I looked at Casey and then back at Heather, and all of a sudden I could see a family resemblance; all of a sudden the explanation clicked. He lived with their father; she lived with their mother. Separate, but tied by blood. Forever.

And watching Casey argue with his sister, I felt nauseous. Here he was, the only guy to ever hold my hand, the only guy I'd ever been able to just talk to and laugh with and be comfortable being *me* around, and he was Heather Acosta's brother.

Her *brother*.

I couldn't deal. I just slid off the stool and headed for the door.

Casey chases after me, calling, "Wait! Sammy, wait!" and comes down the porch steps, saying, "I'm sorry! I haven't seen her all day. I thought she was gone."

I pick up my bike and choke out, "Why didn't you tell me?"

"Tell you what? That she's staying here?"

"No! That you were her brother!"

"But…how could you *not* know that?"

I whip around and say, "All I know about you, Casey, is that you live at 782 Golden Oak Circle, you like skateboarding, mountain biking, skiing, and baseball, and you eat salsa with your macaroni and cheese. You never said your name was Casey *Acosta,* or I might have had a clue. You never called Heather 'my sister,' or hey, I might've known."

"But…"

"But *what?*"

"I don't know…it's not like I was trying to *hide* it from you. So Heather's my sister. She's a pain in the neck, I agree, but *I'm* not Heather."

I didn't know what to say to that. I mean, theoretically he was right. He wasn't Heather any more than Dot was Stan or Troy, but still, my brain was all jumbled up and I was having trouble processing this. It was like the

Huntleys and the Murdocks—it would never be over. Generations from now Keyeses and Acostas would be killing each other, burning down buildings, and plotting revenge. I didn't want that. I wanted to be miles *away* from Heather Acosta, not tied to her.

I shook off the avalanche of thoughts and said, "Look, I've got to go."

"Wait! Why?"

"Because I'm supposed to be spending the day with my friends. Because they're back there, waiting for me. Because I...because I just have to, that's why." I swung onto the bike and tore off down the road. And when I got to the end of Golden Oak Circle and looked back, he'd already gone inside. Inside with his sister.

I tried laughing about it. Tried telling myself that it was just so ironic. So funny. But inside I wasn't laughing. Not at all. And when I passed by Wagonwheel Road and saw the Elephant Truck, I felt downright miserable. Like over the past two days, I'd banged and bruised about every inch of myself on the outside, and now my insides were getting a beating, too.

And I kept telling myself that I shouldn't be so upset. I mean, how long had I known Casey? One whole day. And his best friends *were* Taylor and Jake, and he *did* have the same basic genetic makeup as the person I liked least in the world. And it was clear that he wouldn't be ditching his friends anytime soon, and he could never ditch Heather. Not really.

And the whole time I'm pedaling and brooding about Casey, there's a little thought kind of knocking on the back door of my brain. I know it's there, but it's a door I usually keep locked up tight. But the more I think about Casey and Taylor, the harder it is to keep the door closed.

Finally, it swings open. And standing there, haunting me, is Brandon.

He's there because none of this makes any sense to me. If I'm so weirded out by the fact that Casey likes hanging around with Taylor—a guy who thinks he's so hot, who's manipulative and sneaky and isn't bothered at all by the Edge of the World—then maybe Brandon's somebody I shouldn't trust, either. I mean, Karl is *his* best friend, and from what I've seen and heard, Karl is ten Taylors rolled into one.

By the time I got back to Dot's, my brain felt like overcooked spaghetti. I didn't want to go inside and answer a bunch of questions. I wanted to go someplace, be by myself for a little while, and recover.

But I got lassoed. By Anneke and Beppie. They came out of nowhere with coiled lengths of rope, looped the ends over my handlebars, and started running around, tying me up.

Now you'd think I could handle being ambushed by two little girls, but the minute I'd get Anneke's rope off, Beppie would loop me with hers. And if I'd grab the end of one, they'd just pick up the other end and start using it.

I laughed and said, "Okay! Okay! You got me!" but that just made them giggle and wrap faster and *tighter*. And since part of each rope was hooked around the bike, I couldn't run, I couldn't roll, I couldn't do much of anything but tell them to quit it.

I guess Dot heard me, because she comes crashing out the front door and down the steps, and shoos her sisters off like they're crows in a cabbage patch. They squawk a bit as they're running away, but just like crows, they watch us from a distance and we know—they'll be back.

Marissa and Holly come out and help Dot untangle me, and they're all laughing, saying, "How'd you let them *do* this to you?"

"Don't ask me…those two are…are…"

Dot laughs, "Little monsters, I know." Then she says, "I guess this explains why Stan and Troy never found the rope."

I park Hudson's bike next to the others and ask, "So what are you guys up to?"

Dot says, "We played some more *sjoelbak,* watched Rose Parade reruns, talked about *you*…"

"Yeah. So tell us what happened," Marissa says. "Did you find him? Did you straighten everything out?" and then Holly adds, "I don't see any skateboard…"

Oh yeah. The skateboard. I sighed and said, "You know, I could really use a glass of water."

Dot leads the way up the steps. "Wouldn't you rather have an ice cold root beer?"

"Sure. Whatever."

Holly and Marissa are looking at each other with their eyebrows up, trying not to be too nosy. And they can tell I don't really want to talk about it, but they're dying to ask, so I figure I'll get the whole thing over with. "The bottom line is, Casey has a sister."

Marissa hesitates, then says, "So?"

I sit down at the kitchen table. "Her name's Heather."

At first, it doesn't connect. Then their jaws drop and their eyes pop, and they gawk at me like a row of nutcrackers, waiting to crunch.

Marissa's the first to move. She sits down across from me, leans in, and whispers, *"Acosta?"*

I nod.

Dot moves in beside her. "That is *too* bizarre!"

Holly keeps right on standing. "Was he setting you up? Do they have some kind of genetic predisposition to torture?"

I look at Holly and say, "No. I really don't think so."

Marissa practically shakes the table. "So what *happened?*"

So I tell them. All about the way he'd watched me talk, the things he'd told me about Taylor and his brothers, about being friends and doing drugs and bailing out. Then I tell them how he'd held my hand and pulled me inside, and about Heather, standing in the kitchen in her ratty hair and saggy socks.

And when I'm all done, Marissa and Dot say, "Oh my god. That is just too much!" But Holly's not shocked anymore. She's grinning. Grinning and shaking her head. And when I ask her, "What are you thinking?" she says, "I'm thinking this is perfect."

"Perfect?! How can you say that?"

She leans in and whispers, "Can you think of a better way to torture Heather?"

It was my turn to stare. "Torture Heather? I don't *want* to torture Heather! I just want to be out of her life, and have her stay light-years away from mine."

Holly grins. "Seems to me, you're out of luck."

"No, I'm not!"

Marissa says, "So what are you going to do?"

"I'm going to stay away from him, too, that's what I'm going to do."

"But you *like* him!"

"No, I don't. I don't even *know* him, so how can I like him? Besides, it's too weird. The whole thing is just too weird."

Dot pipes up with, "Yeah. Can you picture Sammy and Heather being sisters-in-law? Or having Heather's mother as a *mother*-in-law? Talk about torture! I can just see them gathered around the table at Thanksgiving, throwing food and yelling. Wow! It would be a mess!"

Well, that gets them going. And while they're busy marrying me off and writing the script for the rest of my life, I get up, get myself a drink of water, and listen. And after my firstborn child has been kidnapped and held for ransom, I can't help it—I bust up. And pretty soon we're all in stitches, crying from laughing so hard.

Then the phone rings. And Dot snatches it up with a giggle, saying, "DeVries." But after a few seconds she's not giggling—she's looking real serious as she holds the phone out to me. "It's Officer Borsch."

We look at each other like, Uh-oh! but what can I do? I take the phone and try to sound calm as I say, "Hello?"

"Sammy?"

"Yeah?"

"I thought you might want to know that Lucinda Huntley's pig is missing."

It took me a second to realize he wasn't calling about stolen blueprints. "Still?"

"So you knew, then. Well, on the 911 tape she sounded very upset, but the sheriff doesn't have the manpower to go chasing after missing pigs. I'd go out there myself, but I'm on duty, and I can't really justify another trip to the boondocks. Especially not for a pig."

"Are you asking *me* to go look for it?"

He hemmed and hawed, and finally he said, "That's up to you."

I laughed and said, "Wow. For a minute there I thought you were actually asking me to *help*."

He laughs, too. "You do have a fertile imagination, don't you?"

"So I've been told." I twist the cord a little and say, "Um...that's all you were calling about?"

I could practically see his eyes pinch. "Should there be something else?"

Me and my stupid mouth. "Well, no. I mean..."

"Sammy...?!"

"No, really. Thanks for letting me know about Penny. I'll try to get over there and help Lucinda look."

I got off the phone before he could ask me any more questions, and when I turned around, there were Dot, Holly, and Marissa, waiting. I smiled at them and said, "Anyone up for a pig hunt?"

Marissa groans, "Oh, please."

"C'mon. It'll be fun. Besides, Officer Borsch says Lucinda's really upset."

So after some moaning and groaning and serious arm-twisting, everyone agreed: We'd go back to Lucinda's *again*, this time to scare up her pig.

What none of us knew—or could ever guess—was just how scared *we* would be, once we got on Huntley property.

TWENTY

Kevin hadn't come home yet, but Lucinda wasn't pacing pine boards over *him*. "Where can she be?" she kept asking. "Where can she *be*? Do you think they stole her?"

We ask, "Who?"

She stops and looks at us. "The Murdocks, of course!"

Dot asks, "Why would the Murdocks want to steal your pig?"

"They've stolen everything else, haven't they? My home, my nephew, why not Penny, too?"

I'd never actually seen anyone wring their hands before, but that's exactly what Lucinda was doing. Back and forth, back and forth, her knuckles stretched and white. She says, "To their eyes, Penny would make a mighty tasty New Year's supper. Those…those… barbarians!"

I'd had enough of watching her fret; I wanted to get out and *look*. "Okay, Lucinda. When's the last time you saw Penny?"

"Right after you left this morning."

"Where was she?"

"Right here. On this very spot. There's only about an hour of daylight left. Oh, I have a horrible feeling. A horrible, horrible feeling."

So I said, "Okay. We'll split up and scour the place. Are there fences anywhere but along the road?"

"All the way around, except for by the ravine."

"So. She's got to be either somewhere on your property, or over on the Murdocks'."

"Oh, she couldn't have made it up the other side of the ravine. That's much too steep for her."

We decided to start on the side of the property opposite the ravine and work our way around the fences—Holly and Dot inspecting the back end of the property while Marissa and I scoured the front end. And after about half an hour of looking in and out, up and down, whistling and calling, "Here, Penny! Come on, girl!" Marissa and I found ourselves at the length of broken fencing where we'd been so many times before.

The sections were still together, and along the bottom of the fence there was only a gap of about six inches. Marissa says, "No way she could squeeze through that…"

I nudged the bottom end, but it didn't flex very much at all. "Nope. No escape there." I looked up and down the road and shook my head. "I wish I knew who's been coming in and out through here. I think it would explain a lot."

"Probably the Murdocks, don't you think?"

"Maybe. But I can't exactly see Chubby and the Darling Damsels *walking* down here, can you? They'd drive, and if they drove, where would they park? Right along here? Everyone would see their car."

Now as I'm talking, I'm looking at an area off the shoulder just across the road. It's your typical section of

Sisquane wilderness—shrubs, oaks, dry grass, and weeds. At least it looks that way, until I notice that there's an area about four feet wide where the weeds are smashed flat.

I pop off the leather strap and wrestle the fence open a few inches, but Marissa grabs my sleeve and says, "Where are you going? I thought we decided she couldn't be out there!"

I point at the road and say, "Look."

"At *what*?"

"At those weeds! C'mon!"

She follows me, but when we get across the street, she says, "Why are you looking at weeds? We're supposed to be looking for a pig!"

I stood at the section of smashed weeds, and straight ahead of me is a sort of tunnel into the shrubs and oaks. "Marissa, look! Do you think a car could fit in there?"

We took a few steps inside. "I think so. Oh, yeah—easy."

Right away my heart sped up. Right away I knew. I whispered, "Marissa, this is where they parked their car."

"Who?"

"Whoever burned down the cabin!"

"You think so?"

I start thinking out loud, saying, "Well, okay. How can we tell if a car's actually been in here?" but I must've been talking to myself, because as I squat down and start checking the bed of oak leaves in the tunnel, Marissa walks off to a different part of the tunnel. And just as I'm confirming that all the leaves in the middle are crushed and the ones on the sides *aren't*, she says, "Sammy! Oh my god, Sammy, come here!"

I drop my crushed-leaf analysis and join her. And there, at her feet, is a cap the size of an old silver dollar.

A shiny cap.

A gas cap.

Marissa whispers, "Do you think…?"

I grab a stick and flip it over. It's red, just like the can had been. And there's not a speck of rust on it. I nod and say, "Absolutely."

She kneels down next to me and whispers, "So what are we going to do?"

"Well, I'm sure not going to leave it here."

Even when she's kneeling, Marissa can do the McKenze dance. "Do you think we're being watched?"

I look around, too. "I don't know. But this time I'm not taking any chances." I pull the sleeve of my sweatshirt down over my hand, pick up the cap, and slip it into my sweatshirt pocket.

Marissa whispers, "Are you going to call Officer Borsch?"

"You bet," I said, then took another look over my shoulders and stood up.

Marissa got up, too, only she says, "Oooo! Oh, what is *that*? Oh, gross! I was kneeling in something."

Now Marissa's jeans are stonewashed to begin with, but since they're her favorites and she wears them every chance she gets, they're extra faded from all the washings. But the stain on her knee isn't *dark,* and I'm about to tell her not to freak out, that it'll wash out, when it hits me.

The spot on her knee is *pink.*

Oaks don't drip pink resins, and no animal on the planet

has pink pee. Not even in Sisquane. And since there's only one liquid I can think of that's pink like that, I squat down, bend over, and sniff Marissa's knee.

She jumps back. "What are you doing? *Smelling* it? Oh, gross, Sammy! What if it's…what if it's…"

I laugh, "Pig pee?"

"Is *that* what you think it is?" Her face crinkles up. "Oh, Sammy, yuck!"

"Marissa! Don't short-circuit on me now. Of course I don't think it's pig pee." I check out the leaves and dirt where she'd been kneeling, but I don't find a thing.

"Then what? God, it's gross. It's like sticking to my knee." She gasps and whispers, "What if it's *blood*?"

"It's way too light to be blood."

"But what if…what if…"

I waddle over toward her and say, "Just hold still, would you?" and take a good whiff of her knee.

"Well?"

I stand up and say, "It's not pee, or blood, or beet juice for that matter—it's transmission fluid."

"Transmission fluid? Like from a car?" She cocks her head. "How would *you* know that?"

"My face took a little bath in it yesterday."

"What?"

"And it washed right off." I smile at her and say, "Your jeans'll come clean. Don't worry about it."

"Wait a minute." She grabs my sleeve as I peek out the tunnel entrance, up and down the road. "You think I'm going to let you off that easy? *When* did your face take a bath in transmission fluid?"

I give her the quick-clip of my little experience under the truck, and of course she turns it into some romantic rendezvous. Then I say, "He's Heather's brother, remember?"

She cringes and says, "Oh, yeah," then switches stations, just like that. "So are you saying you think Ben or *Karl* burned down the house?"

"No! Why would they want to burn down Mary's cabin? I think transmission fluid is like oil. Cars drip it. And whoever parked in those bushes has a car that drips transmission fluid."

"So that could be anybody."

"Well, I don't know. I guess we should see if one of the Murdock cars drips tranny fluid."

Marissa plants herself and puts her hands on her hips. "No. Sammy, I am *not* going back there. N-O, no!"

I keep on walking. "Neither am I. I'm going to tell Officer Borsch about it and ask *him* to go. What I'm really hoping is that he'll be able to lift some fingerprints off this gas cap."

So we're power-walking across the vineyard, and we're almost to the house when Marissa says, "I'm sorry about Casey."

I don't know what to say to that. So instead, I ask something that had been nagging at me ever since I'd peeled myself off the pavement the day before. "Marissa, do you kind of like Taylor?"

"*Taylor?* You've got to be kidding! To tell you the truth, he scares me."

"Really?"

"Yeah. Oh, gross, Sammy. No, I don't like him."

I let out a sigh and say, "Thanks."

"Why? What's the matter?"

"Oh, I don't know. Sometimes I think there's something wrong with *me*."

"What do you mean?"

"I just don't get it about people sometimes. I don't understand Heather and Tenille and why they have any friends at *all*. I don't understand what Casey's doing hanging out with Taylor—even if they have known each other since they were six. And I don't see how in the world Brandon can be best friends with Karl. They seem like opposites to me." I shrug and say, "Maybe I don't know Brandon at all, either."

Marissa's quiet for a minute, then she says, "Well, that's probably true. I mean, he's my cousin, and I don't really know him all that well, so how could you?"

She's right, of course, but something about it really bothers me. Like the better I get to know people, the *less* I know them. Like I can't trust my instincts anymore.

And even though I tried to close the door on that thought, it just would not shut. And the whole time I'm talking to Lucinda about what we'd found and why we needed a Baggie to store the cap in, there it is, pushing back. Even while I'm on the phone to the police, tracking down Officer Borsch, learning that he can't come out to Sisquane for at least another hour, it kept pushing back, harder and harder.

And when I hung up, I held the receiver on the cradle with both hands, closed my eyes for a minute, then gave up. I took a deep breath and asked, "Marissa, what's Brandon's phone number?"

She came around so she could look at me straight on. "Are you serious?"

I nod and look down. "There's something I have to ask him."

She stares at me a minute, but thinks better of cross-examining me. "928-5683," she says, then sits down. Right beside me.

I'm still holding the receiver on the cradle, and I'm telling myself *not* to call him, but I know I'm going to. I have to. I look at Marissa and say, "Can you keep Lucinda company or something?"

She glances over her shoulder at Lucinda, staring out the window. "She's fine. It's you I'm not so sure about."

"I'm fine."

She doesn't budge.

"Marissa!"

"Sammy! He's my cousin and you're my best friend. What don't you want me to hear?"

"It's no big deal, I just want a little privacy, okay?"

"If it's no big deal, then why are you shaking?"

I look at my hands, clamped to the receiver, and say, "I am not!" but there they are, shaking away. Finally, I say, "Oh, good grief," pick up the phone, and dial. And on the fourth ring, a man picks up, so I say, "Hello, is Brandon home? This is Sammy calling."

The voice on the other end says, "Sammy? Really? Hey! What's going on?"

Now, normally when I talk to Brandon, sentences come

out as single words. Usually monosyllabic ones like Yeah and No and Um. But what comes streaming out of my mouth now is, "Not much. Well, actually, that's not true. Marissa and I are at the Huntley house. It's this pioneer place out in Sisquane? Anyway, we're trying to help Lucinda Huntley find her pig. She's like ninety and can't get around too well, and she's really attached to her pig and —"

Brandon interrupts me with a laugh. "You're calling to tell me you're spending New Year's Day finding a pig? Did you want me to come help or something?"

"No, I...actually, that's not why I'm calling at all. See, we're all up here spending the weekend at Dot's new house, and last night we went to the Briggses' party because —"

"You *did*?"

"Well, yeah. Sort of. We weren't actually *at* the party — we just went there to get my skateboard back."

"Your skateboard? How did it wind up at the Briggses' party?"

"It's kind of a long story, but that's not what I wanted to talk about, either."

"Okaaaaaaay..."

"What I want to know is..." I let out a big breath and blurt, "Did you not go to Karl's party because you had somewhere else to go, or because you didn't *want* to go?"

Silence.

"Brandon?"

"Yeah. I'm here."

"I know it's none of my business, but it's kind of important to me."

"Because...?"

"Because it is, okay? I mean, you and Karl are best friends, right? And if he's throwing this big New Year's Eve party, why didn't you go?"

"Were you looking for me there?"

"No! I mean...no!" My cheeks were on fire. "Look, okay. Never mind. I'm kinda confused about some stuff and I really just wanted to know."

"Why I wasn't at the party?"

"Yeah."

Silence. Then, "Sammy, it's kind of complicated. And I'd feel like a rat talking about it."

Suddenly my heart was running away with my breath. "Brandon, look. I saw what was going on in their backyard, and I want to know—does that have anything to do with why you weren't there?"

There was another long silence and then, very quietly, he says, "Let's just say that Karl and I don't have much in common anymore. And since he dropped off the swim team, I really haven't talked to him much."

"But I thought you guys were best friends."

"That's right. We *were* best friends. We're not anymore. He's getting into some heavy stuff, and I just can't go there."

I sat there for a minute, catching my breath. And I can't really explain it, but I was so relieved I started to cry. Water just streamed out of my eyes. And while Marissa's scurrying off to find me a Kleenex or a napkin or something, I'm choking out, "Thanks."

He says, "Are you all right? You're not *crying,* are you? Did something happen over there last night?"

I brush away the tears, then force out a laugh. "Well, I *didn't* get my skateboard, and we *didn't* actually see Ben raging at his brothers, and I *didn't* get arrested, but yeah, I guess you might say a lot happened."

"Whoa now! Re-verse! You gotta fill me in."

So I did. And when I finished the part about Ben yelling at his brothers, he says, "No way that's going to work with Karl *or* Taylor. Ben's got no credibility with either of them after the way he used to tear that house up. I'd go over to Karl's after school, and Ben and this crazy friend of his, Fang, would just be going off."

"Fang?"

"Well, that's what everyone called him. He was Ben's best friend. Anyway, then Dr. Briggs discovered they were growing pot behind the cabaña—and that they were selling it."

"Holy smokes!"

"Exactly. After that everything changed. Dr. Briggs made Ben volunteer at the rehab center in the hospital, and I guess now he wants to be a doctor." He hesitated, then said, "I probably shouldn't be telling you all this, so don't pipeline it, okay?"

"Of course not."

"So what happened after the police showed up?"

"I don't really know because I wasn't there, but Casey says Karl's going to have a police record."

"Taylor's friend Casey?"

"Yeah."

He's quiet a minute, then says, "Maybe I should call Karl. God, what a mess."

So I let him go, but before he hangs up I say, "Brandon?"

"Yeah?"

"Thanks."

"I don't know what I did, but sure." Then he says, "Hey, don't you have a pig to find? You better get hunting—daylight's about gone."

I get off the phone and let out a big sigh. And when Marissa says, "I think you said more to him in the last five minutes than you have in your entire life," I laugh and say, "You're right."

And as we're heading out to resume our search for Penny, it hits me that I'm happy. Really happy. And it's not because I've just talked to Brandon. It's much bigger than that. I'm happy because I feel grounded again. Like I can trust myself.

I wave through the window at Lucinda and call, "Don't worry! We'll find her!" and off we go to find Penny the Pig.

TWENTY-ONE

Dot and Holly had already scoured the back end of the property. No Penny. We filled each other in on what we'd seen and found, then set off to check the last section of property together. And as we're walking along, I'm worried that Marissa's going to start blabbing about how I'd called Brandon, but she doesn't. She just walks beside me, smiling at me from time to time, and I know—my secret's safe with her.

And I'm relieved because it's just too complicated to try to explain. Especially when you're supposed to be looking for a big black pig in the great outdoors—which is almost pitch-black itself.

Holly says, "You know, this is not looking good. We've checked everywhere but the ravine, and I'm not about to go down there in the dark."

Dot says, "Me either. And if we're going to keep searching, I've got to go call my mom and tell her we'll be late for dinner."

Well, really, there was no place else to look. We were standing about ten yards from the cabin fireplace, and even though we could see that Penny wasn't anywhere around the ruins, something was still pulling me in that direction.

Marissa says, "Sammy, I *really* don't want to go over there. It's too creepy!"

"That's okay. You stay here. I just want to take a quick look down the ravine. Maybe she was snorting around and fell in. She went down there before when she found the gas can, you know."

I run over and take a look around, but even with the moon glowing brighter by the minute, I don't see a thing. And as I'm heading back, I can't help but feel that Marissa's right. The fireplace, all scarred and charred, feels creepy. Like something risen from the dead.

I circle the ruins and call out, "No Penny there," but then I hear a snort. I freeze and look around me, calling, "Penny? Penny, was that you?"

Snort, snort!

There's no doubt about it, there's a pig in the vicinity. Trouble is, the snorting sounds a long way away, and I sure don't see her.

I call again, "Penny?!"

Snort, squeal, snort!

Holly runs up, crying, "I heard that! Penny? Penny, here, girl!"

By now we're all looking. Behind trees and rocks and weeds, but we're not *seeing* anything. Finally, Holly says, "Let's just stand together and listen. Then, when she snorts, we'll figure out which direction to go."

So we huddle up about ten feet away from the ruins, and Holly calls, "Penny! Here, girl!"

Squeal, snort! Snort!

Dot points toward a tree and says, "It's coming from

205

over there!" but the rest of us say, "No…it's coming from over *there*," and point straight to the flattened cabin.

Dot laughs and says, "Oh, yeah. I really see a pig over there."

We *were* pointing at ashes and air, but we take two steps in our direction anyway. Dot takes two steps in hers, and then Holly calls again, "Penny? Penny, where are you?"

Nothing.

"Penny? Where'd you go?"

Nothing.

"Penny!"

SNORT!

Dot zooms over to us. And we move forward, but now we're at the edge of the ruins, and really, there's nothing there! Marissa says, "Oh my god, this is just too creepy."

SNORT! Oink, oink, OINK!

Holly says, "It's like she's right here!"

Marissa shivers and starts backing away. "I'm out of here!"

"Marissa! Ghosts don't oink." I pull her back. "There's an explanation, we just have to find it."

Then Holly says, "Look!" so we all scurry over to the edge of the ruins where she is, and there, through large splinters of wood, is a hole. A deep black hole. Holly squats and calls down into it, "Penny?"

SNORT!

Holly smiles at us. "We found her! No one's planning to have her for dinner. She just fell down a hole."

I'm happy about finding Penny, but I just can't help asking, "What's that *hole* doing there? How deep is it?"

We look down it, but we can't tell much—it's totally black. I dig up a pebble, call, "Watch out, Penny!" and let it fall, *clink,* to the bottom.

Marissa says, "That didn't sound like dirt. It sounded like metal," and Dot adds, "But that's not a little hole. It's not a *well,* but it does sound pretty deep."

I tried another one, and this time it landed with a little *thump*.

Holly shakes her head. "That one sounded like it hit dirt."

I get up and say, "Well, we can't tell anything until we get some light down there. I'm going to run back to the house to see if Lucinda's got a flashlight or something."

So I jet off, but when I get to the porch, I can see Lucinda through the window, and she's not alone. Kevin's back. And I want to run up and bang on the door, but I just can't. Kevin's sitting on the edge of a kitchen chair, slumped over, with his face in his hands. And from the way his back is bobbing up and down I can tell— he's crying.

His cowboy hat is sitting on the table next to the blueprints, and Lucinda is standing beside him with her hand on his shoulder, talking to him. She's not yelling, or scolding, she's just talking.

I couldn't interrupt. Even to tell Lucinda that we'd found her pig. So I'm looking around, wondering if maybe there's a flashlight or lantern or something in the toolshed or Kevin's truck, when I remember—Hudson's bike.

I wheel it over to the hole and right away they all groan. I explain about Kevin and Lucinda, and then get busy cranking the pedals. Holly winds up with rear-wheel duty, and Dot stabilizes the front while Marissa looks down the hole. When we get a steady beam of light going, Marissa calls, "I see her! It doesn't look like she can get up...and God, there's a bunch of stuff down there."

I keep cranking and call, "What kind of stuff? How deep is it?"

"I don't know. Bags and pails...a scale..."

I quit cranking. "A *scale*? Let me see that."

So Marissa and I switch. And sure enough there's all *kinds* of stuff down there. Penny's lying at the base of a rickety old ladder leaning against the wall and not far from her are bags and buckets, a fan and a space heater, and then some things that look like they belong in a kitchen — big glass measuring cups, a roll of plastic wrap, a hotplate, a couple of wooden spoons, and a pair of cleaning gloves. And coming right out of the dirt, hanging clear down to the floor, is an extension cord. And at the end of the cord is a power strip, where about six cords could go.

Marissa says, "I can't keep this up much longer, Sammy."

"Just one more minute...I need more light to the left. Can you move a little?" Holly scoots to the right, and that's when I see a bare light bulb with a cord looped around a pipe, which has been hammered into the dirt wall. I look over my shoulder and say, "You can stop now."

Holly lets the back wheel drop. "What is down there?"

Marissa says, "It just looks like an old root cellar with a bunch of junk in it."

I try to find an edge to the board that's been shattered by Penny, but I'm getting covered with soot, and then I get stabbed with a splinter. I cry, *"Owwww,"* yank the spear of wood out of my hand, and say, "Forget this, I'll just go down the way Penny did."

"Go *down?*" Marissa turns me toward her. "You can't go down there!"

"Why not? There's a ladder…it's not that deep…" I give her a little smile and say, "I'll be baaaack!"

I ease my way through the hole, catching the last couple of ladder rungs on the way down. And the first thing that hits me when I land is the smell. It's putrid. Like dirty feet and mildewed sheets, only more chemically than that. I say, "Hi, Penny. Everything's going to be fine," and scoot my feet along the ground so I don't accidentally step on her.

Dot calls, "Are you all right?" and Holly adds, "Sammy, you're not going to be able to lift her—you want me to come down and help?"

I call back, "Give me a minute and I think we'll be able to see what's going on down here."

"How are you going to do that?"

I grope around until I touch the left wall, then find the pipe with the light bulb and follow the cord to its end. Once I've got the plug in my hand, I crawl on the ground, groping along until I find the power strip. I put the two together, and suddenly I'm blinded by light.

I look up, and there's Holly's face with the biggest bug eyes I've ever seen on her. She gasps, "Wow!"

The room isn't big. It's about six feet wide and four feet

long. Max. And there are thick planks, like the ones the cabin had been made of, reinforcing the walls and ceiling. It's like being in a miniature mineshaft.

I go over to Penny and say, "Hi, girl," and check her out. She has a nasty gouge along her belly, and another by her shoulder, but it's her right front leg that's stopping her from getting up. Every time I try to touch it, she squeals and pulls away.

Holly asks, "Is it broken?"

"Looks like it."

"You want me to come down and help you lift her up?"

"It's going to take a lot more than the four of us to get her out of here."

By now Marissa and Dot are looking down the shaft, and Dot says, "What is all that *stuff* doing down there? It looks like Mr. Pence's room!"

It did look like the school's science lab. There was a Bunsen burner, several glass beakers with motorized mixers mounted in them, a jug of denatured alcohol, a bottle of iodine, a box of Hefty bags, and a nearly empty sack of rock salt. But then there was weird stuff, too. Like empty boxes of Sudafed and a graveyard of *drain*-cleaner bottles.

"I have no idea."

Holly says, "Sammy, you've got to get out of there."

Now I had the creeps, too, but I wasn't ready to leave just yet. Then Holly points over in a corner. "Sammy, look! Behind that sack...no, over by the bucket...is that..."

I pull back the sack and say, "...a gas can. Yes, it is."

"Sammy, you've got to get out of there. Now!"

"But I don't get this! Why would the gas can be hidden down here? Maybe it's a different can. Maybe it's..."

All three of them yell, "Sammy! Get out!"

So I'm heading for the ladder when I notice an old scrap of paper sack with something scribbled on it. I pick it up, and what's on it is a list of instructions—so many cups of this mixed with so many ounces of that, stir and heat, cook and cool—it looks like a recipe that's been handed down from generation to generation, only this is not a recipe for biscuits.

No, across the top in faded lead is written METH.

Now the whole time I'd been down there, I wasn't really scared. I mean, sure, I knew being eight feet under in a makeshift cave wasn't *safe*, but I wasn't that worried about it. I was more thinking, What *is* this place? But the minute I figured out what it was, I panicked. I had to get out. Get out *now*.

I charged for the ladder, but my foot caught on the power cord, and as I'm stumbling to the ground, the room goes black.

Holly's voice comes down the shaft. "Sammy! Are you all right?"

I call, "Yeah," because I'm not hurt, but I'm *not* all right. Not at all. I scramble toward the moonlight coming through the hole, and as I hurry up the ladder, I feel bad leaving Penny there, but what else could I do?

And the minute Holly grabs my arm to help me out, does she say, God, I'm glad you're out, or, Why are you shaking so bad? No. She steps back and says, "Oh man! You stink!"

Now, being down there, I'd almost gotten used to the stench. And I tried, but I couldn't really smell it on myself. And as Marissa and Dot take whiffs of me, then crinkle their faces and pull back, I hand Holly the recipe and say, "Like really bad B.O.?"

Even by moonlight, she can read the word METH on the paper. Even by moonlight, I can see the color drain from her face. She chokes out, "Oh my god!"

I'm still shaking. "Exactly."

Marissa says, "What? What are you guys talking about?" but before we can answer, Dot whispers, "Shh! Shh! Listen!"

Sure enough there's the purr of a motor. And it's not along the street or in the Huntleys' driveway. We can't see it, but there's no doubt about it.

Someone's coming.

TWENTY-TWO

We grabbed Hudson's bike and tumbled down into the ravine. And as we're squirming around, getting flat on our stomachs so we can see up over the edge, Dot whispers, "What was that paper about? Why are we hiding? Why are you and Holly so freaked out?"

I whisper back, "That's a drug lab down there." I hold up the paper. "This is a recipe for methamphetamine."

She says, "What?! But who...," and Holly and I say at the same time, "Dallas!"

Dot says, "Oh, you've got to be kidding!"

"There he is, right now!"

Dallas doesn't have his headlight on. He just putts up, rolls his motorcycle beside an oak, and parks. Then he takes a flashlight out of one of his saddlebags and turns it on, but the beam is muted. Like it's on a dimmer. He sort of sneaks over to the rubble, but as soon as he sees the hole in the plywood, he switches off the light and hurries back to his bike.

He stands behind the oak tree for the longest time, waiting and watching. And while he's waiting and watching, we're barely breathing, trying to shrink into the hillside.

Finally, he decides to risk it. He tiptoes over to the shaft, then slides the plywood aside, just like that. He takes one last look around, switches on his flashlight, and then stays there for a minute, crouched over the hole.

Penny lets out a great big *SNORT!*, and after he tries to quiet her with *"Shh! Shh!"* he mutters something about stupid nosy pigs and disappears into the ground.

The minute he's out of sight, Marissa whispers, "What are we going to *do?*" and Dot says, "You think he's mixing up metha…whatever that stuff is…right *now?*"

"No," I say, "I think he's getting his supplies out, so he can mix it up someplace else."

Holly says, "That sneaky lowlife! He's so sorry for Lucinda. Right! He doesn't care squat about the cabin, he just wants the cover!"

Marissa shakes her head. "I don't understand…did *he* burn it down?"

I whisper, "No."

"Then what's the gas can doing down there?"

"Oh, he put it there, all right, because he didn't want anyone to find out who did."

All three of them look at me and say, "What?" and Dot adds, "What kind of sense does *that* make?"

I could barely keep up with how fast the pieces were clicking together. "Let's put it this way—I don't think the Murdocks burned down the house. Or Kevin or that real-estate rattlesnake or the developers or the *Snout,* for that matter. I think the person who burned down the cabin knows Dallas, and he knows Dallas is a dealer."

"Who?" They look at me like a family of owls.

"Ben."

Dot says, *"Briggs?"*

"That's right."

Marissa says, "Oh, Sammy. That is so out there!"

"Maybe. And maybe not. Look, Ben used to be addicted to meth. He owns a truck that he bought from Dallas. There's transmission fluid over there in the tree tunnel where we found the cap. We know Ben's truck leaks tranny fluid and..."

"But you said—"

"I know, I know, that it's like oil—all cars drip it. But there are just too many connections here."

Marissa says, "I don't know. They seem to be pretty weak connections to me."

"But hang on. Have you noticed that necklace Dallas wears? You know what's hanging from the middle of it?"

Holly nods. "It's a tusk or a tooth."

"Right. A *fang*. Brandon told me that Ben used to have this really wild best friend that everybody called Fang."

Dot says, "*Brandon*? When did you talk to him?"

"I'll tell you about it later. What matters now is the connection. Add to that the fact that all of the Briggs brothers have used meth and that Dallas has probably had some sort of run-in with the law before..."

Dot says, "Where do you get *that*?"

"The first time Holly and I met Dallas he said something about being grateful to her for giving him a chance when no one else would...like he had a record or something. Anyway, if you put all those things together, the connection starts getting a little stronger."

Dot's still shaking her head. "So why's Ben want to go and burn down the house?"

215

"Because his ex–best friend is supplying drugs to his little brother and he's going to stop him any way he can. Maybe he followed Dallas and figured out he was making drugs here. Maybe he wanted to *kill* him—who knows? All I know is there's a lot more to this than we can guess, but there's a connection—a strong one."

Holly whispers, "Okay. Let's say you're right. It still doesn't answer, What are we going to do? Right here. Right now."

They all look at me like, Yeah—what are we going to do? And I feel like telling them, How should *I* know? but instead I put a finger up to my lips and nod out at the ruins.

Dallas comes up slowly, and he pulls a Hefty sack along with him. It's not full, but it's jingling and clanging with the weight of what's inside. He sneaks over to his motorcycle, and at first he tries to put some of the stuff inside a saddlebag, but decides to forget that. He's just going to tie the bag to the bike and haul his chemistry set off that way.

When he's satisfied that he's got the Hefty bag secure, he takes another look around and heads back for a second load.

Holly says, "We've got to do something!"

I say, "Well, Officer Borsch is supposed to be here pretty soon."

"That doesn't help us now!"

"You want to let some air out of his tires?"

Holly says, "No. He'll see it and know someone's on to him."

Dot whispers, "Yeah. Don't drug dealers carry guns and knives and stuff? What if he decides to *kill* us?"

Marissa's shaking her head. "I say we make a break for it. Go to the house, call the police, maybe get *Kevin* out here..."

They're right and I know it, but I just don't want to leave. "What if he takes off? What if he *hears* us? What if..."

"What if we trap him?" Holly's smiling. Like she's got a plan. "Let's put the board back on and trap him inside."

Dot says, "But there's a big *hole* in the board!"

Holly's still smiling. "So let's put Sammy's bike on top of the board."

I'm getting her picture. "Lay it flat?"

"Yeah!"

It flashed through my brain that this was not *my* bike, but I didn't want Sisquane's very own drug lord to weasel out of what he'd been doing. I wanted to trap him. Red-handed.

Marissa shakes her head. "Dot's right. Drug dealers *kill* people."

Dot says, "But if you leave the cage open, you may never catch the bird."

Marissa says, "What?"

"Just a Dutch expression."

"So you're with *them*? I can't believe it. You guys are crazy!"

I say, "I think we should do both. The three of us trap him inside, and you go get Kevin and Officer Borsch."

Holly whispers, "Well, if we're going to move, we'd

better *move*. I'm surprised he hasn't come up already."

So Holly and I scurry over as quietly as we can while Dot and Marissa carry Hudson's bike. Holly takes one end of the board and I take the other, and just as we're getting ready to slide it on, we see Dallas coming up the ladder, a Hefty bag slung over his shoulder.

He sees us, all right, and at first he freezes. Then, when he realizes what we're about to do, he drops the bag and comes charging at us.

We slam the board in place, stand on either end of it, and cry, "Now! Put it on now!" to Marissa and Dot.

They get all kind of tangled up moving the bike around, and then practically throw the thing on us. And it's way too late when we realize that Holly's plan is not going to work. The bike won't lie flat because the pedal's in the way.

Marissa takes off for the house like a shot, and we can see Dallas through the hole just looking at us.

Now while we're banging around trying to get the bike in place, he's not pushing on the board or yelling at us or anything. Instead, he's sort of laughing, saying, "What do you girls think you're doing?"

The last thing I want to do is talk to the Sisquane Connection, so I don't say a word. I just keep on wrestling with Hudson's bike, struggling to get a better seal on the hole. He says, "Hey, I don't know what you're thinking, but I found Penny down here and she's hurt. There's also a bunch of really weird stuff stored here, which we ought to ask Kevin about. Hey, come on. Let me out. This is giving me the creeps!"

He sounds so calm. So reassuring. So completely unfazed. And for a second there I thought that maybe I was wrong. Then the pedal snaps into the hole, leaving the rear wheel flat and the hole sealed up.

He takes the pedal and turns it, whipping the tire around faster and faster until the spokes are like a blaze of chrome in the moonlight. "Gee. Isn't this fun?"

I stomp on the tire with my high-top and say, "We're not stupid, you know. That's your little drug lab, and we know it."

He laughs, "Drug lab? Are you serious? It looks like a bunch of junk to me. Maybe Kevin used this for storage a long time ago. Come on…I'll go with you and ask him about it."

Dallas' voice is still calm, but he's starting to push up on the board. And even though pushing from a ladder doesn't give you the best leverage, he's not just playing. He wants *out*.

Holly says, "Tell it to the judge, buddy. We're not letting you out until there's a squad of policemen here to escort you to jail."

All of a sudden the pushing stops, and two seconds later the blade of a shovel comes gashing through the spokes of Hudson's bike. "Let me out!" he growls, then pries the shovel back down, snapping a gap in the spokes. Dot shrieks and jumps back, and for a second we all let up on the bike. He pushes the wheel up, but the pedal catches on the plywood and it doesn't quite come off the hole.

I jump on the wheel with both feet, but it doesn't go back down right, and I spin around and fall, like I missed my step on a merry-go-round. Holly jumps on right after me, and there goes the wheel, *snap,* into place.

It's quiet for about ten seconds, and then the spade comes crashing through the spokes again like Jaws from under water. Holly skips to the side, so I jump back on the wheel while Dot holds down the frame. There comes that spade, gashing through again. And again. And every time it goes back under, it destroys a piece of Hudson's bike.

So I'm dancing on this disintegrating merry-go-round, feeling sick about Hudson's bike, panicking because I don't know what in the world is taking Marissa so long, when the spade shoots up and gashes right through *me* on its way back down. My jeans are torn, my leg is gouged, and pain is screaming through my body.

And all of a sudden I'm mad. I'm still scared for my life and nauseous from the pain, but running over my emotions like an eighteen-wheeler is anger. Pure, hot anger. And even though I had nothing to fight with, I wanted to hurt him back. Pound on him. Gouge him. Bury him alive.

I start scooping up handfuls of dirt. Of ashes. And I drop them through the spokes and cry, "You're a dirtbag, you hear me? A dirtbag! And if you think we're going to let you out of there so you can go make drugs someplace else, you don't know your grave from a hole in the ground. You hear me? You're dead. D-E-A-D, dead! You're a lowlife, blood-sucking *creep,* and we're going to *bury* you, you hear me? Bury you!"

There's no way a few handfuls of dirt and ash are going to fill in a root cellar. I knew it was like throwing sand at the ocean, but I was so mad at him that I couldn't stop. And I wasn't just mad at him for gouging me up and destroying Hudson's bike, or for deceiving Lucinda into thinking she'd seen Moustache Mary's ghost. No, it was finally sinking in—really sinking in—just exactly who Dallas Coleman was.

He wasn't the foreman for Huntley Vineyards. He wasn't the hand who worked for no pay. He wasn't nice or caring or friendly. He was evil. Sneaky, calculating, and evil.

And the more I saw him for exactly what he was, the more anger I felt for what he did down there. For the poison he made. For the lives he ruined. And I couldn't stop myself—I was flinging dirt and ashes on him like my life depended on it.

Then the strangest thing happens.

He stops fighting.

I stand there for a minute, shaking, and then from the darkness below us comes coughing. Cussing and coughing. Dot whispers, "Oh, Sammy, listen…you got it in his *eyes!*" She says, "Yes!" and starts tossing in dirt, too.

The cussing stops, and so does the coughing. And then all of a sudden, like a ghoul from a grave, his hand shoots up and grabs my ankle. And before I can stop him, he's twisted my foot through the shattered spokes of Hudson's bike, and there's nothing I can do.

I'm going down.

TWENTY-THREE

Dot shrieks, "Oh my god!" and Holly yells, "Kevin! Marissa! HELP!"

Dallas is twisting and pulling so hard that it feels like my leg is going to be sliced like bologna by the spokes of the wheel. And even though I won't fit through the opening in the spokes, it feels like he's going to drag me under, if he has to kill me to do it.

I keep moving and pulling back, trying to get free. But the pain is making me sick to my stomach and I'm feeling really light-headed. Then my vision starts blurring and I can barely breathe, and Dot's voice, as she screams for help, is like a whisper in the distance. Suddenly Holly kneels beside me with a broken-off spoke in her hand. "Here! It's all I could find...Sammy, stab him!"

I choke out, "You."

"I can't see what I'm doing! I'll probably stab *you!*"

I take the spoke from her, and it feels small. Like a twelve-inch needle. But when I lean forward, I can see Dallas' hand, his arm, wrenching my calf. I hold my breath, aim, and stab with all my might. Two seconds later my foot is free, and let me tell you, that's not Penny down there wailing like a stuck pig.

I pull my leg out of the hole, and when Dot shouts, "They're coming! They're coming! And Officer Borsch is with them!" I'm so relieved that I practically break down and cry.

Then the earth explodes. Hudson's bike and the shattered board fly up, and Dallas shoots out of the pit like a demon from the underworld, looking like he's going to tear off our heads and rip us to shreds.

And he might have, only Kevin tackled him first. And even though Dallas flipped and whipped and acted like a shark on a pier, Kevin managed to get his hands behind him, and Officer Borsch didn't waste any time snapping handcuffs on him.

And you'd think at this point Dallas would just give up, but he doesn't. Even with a gun between his shoulder blades, he keeps tugging and kicking until Kevin whips the rope from the loops of his jeans and wraps him up like a rodeo calf.

Officer Borsch says, "Let's secure him in the squad car," to Kevin, then takes a quick peek into the hole with a flashlight. Five seconds later he turns to me and says, "This is a clan lab! Back up! All of you, back up! This place may be booby-trapped." Then he looks back down the shaft and says, "How'd that *pig* get down there?"

Well, Penny must've heard his voice, because she starts oinking and snorting and carrying on like the world is coming to an end. I laugh and say, "She fell in, and I don't think she wants you to leave her there."

"Well, that's exactly what we're going to do until the investigators get here." He looks at me, standing right beside him. "Stand *back*, Sammy! How many times do I have to tell you?"

"It's not booby-trapped, Officer Borsch."

"How do you know that? Just because the pig didn't set it off doesn't mean there's not a trip cord around here. Back up, would you? Just back up!"

I back up to make him happy, but while I'm moving, I say, "Dallas went down there, Penny went down there, and I went down there. It's not booby-trapped."

He whips around. "*You* went down there?"

"Yeah. I didn't know what it was. Not until I found this." I hand him the recipe.

He takes one look at it, grabs me by the shoulders, and says, "Sammy, you could've been *killed*. Cookers don't play around. They set cyanide traps and rig up ether bombs. They'd kill you as soon as look at you!"

I'm starting to get the picture. And I'm about to say something real profound like, I didn't know…when I see Lucinda shuffling toward us.

Right away I know that the pain I'm feeling in my leg doesn't compare to the one in her heart. But she stops Kevin and Officer Borsch from hauling Dallas to the car, then stands as tall as she can and says to Dallas, "You've deceived me, you've betrayed my trust, and you've destroyed Mary's home. But I'm a Huntley, and that's something you can't take from me. I'll always be the descendant of a fine, upstanding, courageous woman who will be remembered with honor and reverence for her strength and her accomplishments. You, young man, have set your own legend into motion, and I pity those who are condemned to recall it."

Dallas looks to the side, and all he can say for himself is, "I didn't burn it down."

"What you did is much worse." She turns her back on him, then shuffles over to us, saying, "Would one of you be so kind as to go to the house and wait for Dr. Pele? He's agreed to take a look at Penny, but he won't know where to find us. I'd wait for him myself, but I don't want to leave Penny."

Officer Borsch calls, "You keep her away from that pig! Sammy? Do you hear me? Stand back from that shaft. Farther! Sammy, help me out here! I've got to get this creep put away and get the investigators out here to dismantle that lab, and I don't have time to baby-sit stubborn women!" I point to myself like, Who? Me? and he yanks Dallas along and calls, "Yes, you!" Then he looks at the others and says, "And you, and you, and you, and you! You headstrong females are going to be the death of me!"

So Officer Borsch and Kevin haul Dallas away, and Dot decides she'll go to the house to wait for the vet and call her mom. Marissa goes with her, which leaves Holly and me with Lucinda, the moon, and a sky full of stars.

At first Lucinda *is* stubborn. She wants to see Penny, and she's not in the mood to wait for someone to haul her out of the cellar. But we make her sit down on a felled tree trunk, and then sit beside her, one on each side.

And at first Lucinda's full of questions. She wants to know everything. But after a little while we find ourselves just sitting there, staring at the ruins, at the stone fireplace poking up from the earth. And Lucinda says, "I never considered myself to be someone who was living in the past, just appreciative of it." She gets a faraway look in her eye. "I never thought I'd leave—certainly never thought I'd be forced out. If only we hadn't fallen on such hard times..." She shakes her head and sighs. "Poor Kevin. All this time he's been trying to protect me from how bad things really are."

Holly whispers, "Does this mean you have to sell?"

Lucinda's eyes are brimming with tears. "Do you know why Kevin was at the Murdocks' today? To tell them no. To tell them they had gone too far, burning down Mary's house, and that he wanted no part in any dealings with them."

"You mean he didn't know what they were planning?"

She sighs and says, "Last June I was deathly ill, and Kevin saw no sense in continuing the vineyard. He got approached about this development idea and didn't think it would hurt to have a few sketches made, but they took that as permission to go hog wild. I don't blame him for what he did, but it breaks my heart to think of these magnificent oaks being cut down...the thought of sod and golf carts and *condominiums*. It seems so artificial, so *smooth*. There's something about the rugged outdoors that makes you feel a part of the world around you." She lets out another sigh. "Oh, I don't know. It's a different time, and humans are a different breed. Life's become entertainment where it used to be an experience."

We're all quiet for a minute, then Holly asks, "So what are you going to do?"

"The truth is I have no choice. We've fallen into debt, and since I can't come up with a better solution, I suppose we'll have to sell the property."

Holly whispers, "What about Mary? What about the house?"

"The house is gone, but Mary? Mary will never be gone. As long as there's her diary to read, people will know her. And remember her."

I was about to tell her that that was true. Mary Rose Huntley was not somebody *I* could forget anytime soon. Neither was Lucinda. But before I can, Lucinda says, "Dallas probably discovered that root cellar when he was searching for the gold."

Holly says, "Hey...do you think *he* found it? Do you think it was hidden down there?"

"Hmmm," Lucinda says, like she hadn't even considered it. "I rather doubt it. A scoundrel like that wouldn't stick around if he'd discovered it. Besides, it makes no sense against the riddle. The ridge is nowhere near it."

As I'm listening to Lucinda, looking at the moon shining on the chimney of the fireplace, something in my brain snaps. Hard. And all of a sudden my heart starts beating faster and I'm feeling very strange. I whisper, "The ridge. The *ridge*."

She says, "It's no use, my dear. I've looked all my life. We've dug up every square foot of land anywhere near the ridge." She lets out a long, choppy sigh. "The gold was either discovered long ago, or perhaps Mary used it herself."

Now while she's talking, I'm walking over to the chimney like a zombie saying, *"Where the ridge meets the rock and the rock meets the ground..."*

Holly jumps up and follows me. "Where are you going?"

"To where the ridge beam of the roof met the rock of the chimney."

Lucinda shuffles behind us. "The ridge *beam*? Why, I'm sure that's not what she meant..."

I just keep moving, then stand by the fireplace and say, "The ridge beam rested right in that big notch in the rock. See it? The ridge beam meets the rock of the chimney...and the stones go all the way to the ground!"

"Yes, but..."

"And Lucinda! The box! How's that part go? *The box is shallow, black and crowned...?*"

"That's right, but..."

"Lucinda, this is it! It has to be! The *fire* box is not very deep, it's black from soot, and crowned—you know, arched!"

Lucinda had quit arguing. She was right alongside us, saying, "*Not far in, left and high...Gold and silver, warm inside.* Warm from the fire! Oh, girls! After all these years. It's been right here in front of me!"

Holly says, "But *where*?"

Lucinda's all over it. She ducks her head in, facing the left side of the fireplace, and runs her bony fingers over the rocks, shaking them one by one. Suddenly she freezes, then turns to us and whispers, "I believe this one's loose. Girls, come help me lift it out!"

There wasn't room for the three of us, but there was no way Lucinda was leaving. So we worked around her, and sure enough there was a loose stone. We wiggled and tugged, and when we got it to budge, soot and sand dusted into our eyes. We didn't care, though, we just squinted and tugged until we had the stone pulled free.

Lucinda whispers, "Is there anything back there?"

I wanted to jam my arm in and feel around, but it wasn't right. I said, "Go on, Lucinda. You look."

She reaches inside, and for a moment she just freezes with her arm inside the wall. Then she pulls out a thick leather satchel about half the size of one of the fireplace stones and holds it to her chest for a moment, her hands shaking. Then she kneels on the ground, pulls open the drawstring, and giggles like a six-year-old. "We found it! We *found* it!"

She loosens the drawstring completely, then pulls out a handful of very old, very gold coins. And when she looks up at us, she's got tears streaming down her face. She says to the sky, "Thank you, Mary," then smiles at us and whispers, "Thank you, girls."

And with the moonlight on her face as it's turned up to look at us, she doesn't seem like she's nearly a century old. She looks full of life. Almost young. And even though there's no doubt in my mind that she'll always be the Lucinda I've come to know—she'll still walk her pig and peek in coffins if that's what she has a mind to do—I can tell that from this point on, things are going to be different.

Very different.

TWENTY-FOUR

It didn't take long for the place to be swarming with cops. And parked in the middle of all those squad cars was one big green delivery truck. The police took our statements, one by one, while Mr. and Mrs. DeVries hung around looking very worried.

Dot asks them, "Where are Anneke and Beppie?"

Mrs. DeVries says, "The boys are looking after them," and Mr. DeVries adds, "Stan and Troy were very anxious to come along, but we didn't think it would be a good idea if we *all* came. You'll have to tell them about it when we get home, *ja?*"

Dot grins and says, "Sure," and you can tell she's thinking that no ghost story of theirs could ever top her real-life story.

When we finally do get to the DeVrieses', the rest of us are completely talked out and very hungry. So while Dot holds court with her brothers and sisters, Marissa and Holly help Mr. DeVries whip up a plate of *hamburgers,* of all things, and Mrs. DeVries helps me clean my hurt leg.

Even after she was done patching me up, she kept insisting that I go to a doctor. But Grams wasn't going to be home for another day, and since doctors are expensive and I wasn't sure about our insurance, I didn't know what to do. Besides, nothing was broken and I didn't *want* to go to one.

So we ate our hamburgers and settled on Hudson's. I told them he was a retired doctor and that he'd patch me up just fine. And who knows? Maybe he is. He had supplies, and when I called, he said I was welcome, and that's all I really cared about.

Then Marissa and Holly confessed that they'd really like to collapse in their own beds, so Dot helped us pack our stuff, and we piled everything in the back of Mr. DeVries' delivery truck.

After we dropped off Marissa, we drove to Cypress Street, and there was Hudson, waiting on the porch. Mr. DeVries carried Hudson's bike up the steps and leaned it against the railing, and after the two of them discussed doctors and dressings and disinfectants for a while, Mr. DeVries set off to deliver Holly.

So there we were, alone on the porch—Hudson, me, and his mangled bike. And really, he didn't say a word about it, but he couldn't help looking at it. I cringed and said, "I'm so sorry, Hudson. I'll buy you a new one."

He examined it, then said, "*How* did you manage this?"

I started to tell him. About Lucinda and the cabin, and what it had meant to her. About Moustache Mary crossing the plains and the longstanding rivalry between the Huntleys and the Murdocks. And I'm barely getting warmed up when he says, "Whoa! Whoa, young lady!" and for a second there I'm thinking he's going to say, The *bike*...would you tell me about the *bike*? but instead

231

he grins at me and asks, "Does this story require a cup of cocoa?"

I laugh and say, "Oh, Hudson, it's going to take a whole vat!"

So we go inside and he makes us some hot chocolate, and then we sit down at the kitchen table and I tell him everything. Everything. And when I get to the part about the Briggses' party and the Edge of the World, he's looking worried. Almost angry. And I tell him that the Edge of the World really bothers me because it seems like one day you're over here with your friends and everything's fine...and then suddenly there you are at the Edge of the World. I shake my head and ask him, "How does that *happen*?"

He just nods. Very seriously. And finally he says, "By degrees. It happens by degrees. A little deviation in direction often takes you from where you *wanted* to go right to the Edge of the World." He nods some more, then says, "And I don't think it's really an edge, because if it were, more people would recognize it and give thought to the steps they're taking. It's more a gradual slope down. An easy path to take. But once you start down, the momentum builds, and you have a difficult time stopping and pulling yourself back up."

When we get done talking about the Edge of the World, I tell him about the rest of the party. About Casey. About him being Heather's brother. And when Hudson tries to tell me that, really, the fact that Casey is Heather's brother doesn't have to have anything to do with Casey being my friend, I stop him cold and say, "Look at the

Murdocks and the Huntleys! I don't want a life like that! I don't want to worry that Heather's going to come gunning for me, or that she's going to kidnap and torture my children."

"What?"

I laugh and say, "Never mind. You had to be there." I take a sip of cocoa and add, "Besides, Casey doesn't see much scary about the Edge — or the Slope, or whatever you want to call it — or that his friends are already on their way down."

Hudson pulls on an eyebrow and says, "Maybe no one's ever pointed out the terrain to him."

"Whatever. I'm staying out of it."

He eyes me and asks, "So what happened with that skateboard of yours? Did you get it back?"

I pout and say, "No. Casey still has it."

He gives me a little smile and says, "Aaah." That's all, just "Aaah."

"Stop that!"

He's still grinning. "More cocoa?"

"No, what I want to do is explain why your bike's a mess so I can go soak my body. I ache all over."

So I tell him about the root cellar in Moustache Mary's cabin being converted into a drug lab and about the Elephant Truck connection. And then I tell him about trapping Dallas in the pit, and the way he almost killed me trying to get out.

And when I'm all done, Hudson takes a deep breath and says, "The bicycle was certainly a small sacrifice for your well-being."

"It was stupid. *I* was stupid. I guess I should have known that he'd go berserk, but I didn't. Anyway, I promise, Hudson, I'll get you another bike."

He winks at me and says, "I knew there were risks when I lent it to you, and I did tell you not to worry about it, so don't. Maybe we'll rebuild it as a project together, but for now, why don't you go take that bath?"

So I went to take a soak, but when I saw myself in the bathroom mirror, I had to take a minute and stare. From the bruise on my forehead to the gouge in my leg, I looked like I'd been through a war. I didn't feel any wonderful sense of victory, though. I was just pummeled. And tired.

After my bath, when Hudson was helping patch me up, he said, "At a very minimum, you're going to get a tetanus shot tomorrow," and since I was too tired to argue with him, I just said, "Yeah-yeah-yeah," and crashed on his couch.

I probably would've slept until noon, but at around eight in the morning there's this little *tap-tap-tap* on the front door, and when Hudson answers it, I know who's there. I can hear him asking for me. And right away I panic because I don't know how in the world Officer Borsch could have known I was there.

I get dressed as fast as I can and rake my fingers through my hair, and then stuff my things out of sight—just like I do at home. And I can hear Officer Borsch saying, "Well, I noticed the bike on the porch and..."

I step up to the front door, beside Hudson. "Officer Borsch! How's it going?"

He doesn't have to answer. I can see how it's going. He's a complete mess, and the bags under his eyes are huge. Even for the Borsch-man. So before he can answer, I say, "Good grief. What happened?"

Hudson interrupts. "Would you like to come in? I can brew you some coffee or…"

"No, no. Thank you, sir. There are just a few things I'd like to tell Samantha." He eyes the porch, and Hudson picks up on the fact that Officer Borsch would probably be more comfortable talking to me alone. So Hudson says, "Well, sure. You two have a seat out here. I've got an appointment to go jogging in about fifteen minutes anyway, so just make yourselves at home."

I wanted to grab Hudson and say, "Hey, wait a minute! What's with this jogging bit?" but the door's already closing on us.

So we sit down on the porch, and it feels kind of strange, having Officer Borsch planted in Hudson's chair. I mean, there's no way he would ever listen to me the way Hudson does, but still, there he was, sitting in Hudson's chair like he belonged.

He takes a deep breath and says, "It's been a long night, Sammy. But the investigators have dismantled the clan lab, and even though they've still got to test the property for toxic waste, it's pretty much cleaned up."

"Did Dallas run that extension cord from the toolshed? I was trying to figure that out after we left."

"That's right. He just ran a trench and buried it." He shakes his head and says, "Clan labs aren't usually too sophisticated, but Coleman's was real makeshift."

"Why's it called a clan lab? I mean, it was just him, right? Not a whole clan."

He tries not to smile. "Clan as in clandestine. But you're right. Mr. Coleman's operation was small. Generally there are at least a few people involved."

"So did you get anything out of Dallas?"

"What do you mean?"

"Did he talk?"

"Like a clam." He smiles again. "But you were on the spot with that Briggs boy. I didn't have the chance to get details from you last night, but I'd sure like to know how you pieced that one together."

So I tell him about the Elephant Truck and the transmission fluid and the gas cap. And then about what I'd seen and heard at the party and what I'd learned from Brandon and Casey. And I don't know if it was the porch or the chair or what, but for once Officer Borsch didn't interrupt me or roll his eyes. He just listened.

When I was all done, I asked, "Do you think Dallas put the gas can in the cellar so people wouldn't know that it was arson and start investigating?"

"More than that. He used it to blackmail Ben Briggs. He caught Briggs leaving the scene and confronted him in that oak tunnel where you found the lid to the gas can. They had a scuffle, but when Coleman realized what Briggs had done, he ran off to try and save the cabin. Later he told Briggs that if he caused him any more trouble, he'd turn him in. Briggs was petrified because Coleman made it sound like he'd destroyed a priceless historic monument—not just an old shack.

"By the way, you were right about them being best friends, and that Coleman selling meth to the youngest boy was what lit Briggs' fuse. Briggs says he followed Coleman for a week, finally made the connection that he was cooking in the shack, and decided to destroy the operation."

"What's going to happen to Ben?"

Officer Borsch sighs. "Miss Lucinda doesn't want to press charges."

"You're *kidding*."

He shakes his head. "She sees no sense in it." He eyes me and says, "That woman reminds me a lot of you."

"Me? Lucinda?" I think about that a minute and say, "Well, thanks."

"Not that I want to see you walking a pig anytime soon…"

"Oh! So what happened to Penny?"

He laughs. "What a life. Anyone else would've turned her into bacon. Not Lucinda Huntley."

"What happened? How'd you get her out?"

"With a tow truck. They put a sling on the hoist and pulled her out oinking and squealing."

I laughed at the thought. "What about her leg?"

"Lucinda's convinced her vet to set it. I've never heard of such a thing, but there you have it. She's going to take the pig for walks in a *wagon* until the leg's better." He shakes his head and says, "Don't ask me how she's going to pull the thing—I don't know."

I laugh, too, and say, "If I know Lucinda, she'll find a way."

He stands up and says, "Well, I'm glad I noticed the bike. I was on my way in, and I thought—well, I thought you might want to know." He takes a deep breath and shakes his head at the bike. "It's a shame. That one was a classic."

I stand next to him with my hands on my hips and nod. "Yeah. Hudson's *real* glad he lent it to me."

Officer Borsch rubs the stubble on his chin. "We don't have anything *vintage* like this...but how about a mountain bike? Could your friend handle one of those?"

"Hudson?" I laugh and say, "Oh, he can handle anything." Then I turn to him and ask, "But what are you saying?"

He hikes up his gunbelt and says, "I can't promise anything yet, but it seems the least the department could do." He smiles at me. "Line of duty and all that."

Now I probably can't explain this right, but let's just say that at that moment I felt like Officer Borsch had pinned a DEPUTY star on me. And bike or no bike, I felt like I'd just grown two inches. I smiled at him and said, "That's a nice thought, anyway."

He goes down the porch steps and says, "Let me see if I can make it happen."

He gets in his car and zooms off, and then Hudson comes zipping out of the house in sweats and tennies, saying, "Go inside and get some more shut-eye. I'll be back in a bit," and disappears down the street.

So there I am, on the morning of the second day of a brand-new year, on Hudson's porch, alone with my thoughts. And I play it all through my brain again like a movie. And when I finish the rerun, I think about the path I walk with my friends. About how lucky I am to have Marissa and Dot and Holly.

Then I think about Dallas and Ben. About Karl and Brandon, Heather and Tenille. About Taylor and Snake and Casey. And it's funny—in my mind, I can see the forks in their roads, their cliffs and their valleys, but when it comes to *my* path, I see nothing.

And in a way, that bothers me. I mean, I have no idea what I want to do. Where I want to go. What I want to be. I've always just lived day to day, school year to summer.

But sitting there on Hudson's porch with the sun shining over the neighbors' rooftops, I remember Officer Borsch comparing me to Lucinda. And it hits me that Lucinda is as much like Mary Rose Huntley as anyone could be, and that nothing, *nothing,* had stopped Mary. She wasn't a curse. She was just determined. Determined to stay on her own path regardless of how hard others tried to throw her off.

And suddenly I'm flushed with this strong, very powerful sense that no matter where I decide to go, no matter what I decide to be, if I can stay on my own path and not let floods or droughts or wild redheads stop me, I am going to make it.

Even if I have to put on a moustache somewhere along the way.

Wendelin Van Draanen has been everything from a forklift driver to a high school teacher and is now enjoying life as a full-time writer. The first four books in the Sammy Keyes mystery series have been embraced by critics and readers alike, and *Sammy Keyes and the Hotel Thief* received the 1999 Edgar Allan Poe Award for best children's mystery.

Ms. Van Draanen lives with her husband and two sons in California. Her hobbies include the "three R's": reading, running, and rock 'n' roll.